ASPEN HEIGHTS

For Rachelle's parents and sisters who are always there for her. To Will's Mom, Sister and Aunt for all they have done for him.

ASPEN HEIGHTS

Rachelle Graham

Will Romero

3

Aspen Heights
Best Friends

Published by the Best Friend's group
Copyright 2015 @ Rachelle Graham Will Romero
All Rights Reserve
Printed in the United States of America

ASPEN HEIGHTS

Rachelle Graham

Will Romero

Chapter One

A blood-red Mercedes driven by none other than Mercedes headed right towards me. My life didn't flash before my eyes; rather my bloody limbs and guts landed on the cold, hard concrete.

Oh wait, was that my imagination

"Stay off the sidewalk, bitch. Just because you're named after one doesn't mean you can drive one?" Cherry yelled as she pushed me out of the way and into the bushes, risking her own life in the process.

I wish her yelling was also part of my imagination. Mercedes was the second most popular girl in school and I did not want her hating us anymore than she already did.

Trying to run us over did show some pure hate though.

Realizing I was safe, just covered in sticky painful bushes. I said, "Shhh, she's going to hear you."

"Yeah, that's kind of the point," Cherry flipped off the back of the fast-moving vehicle.

"She's going to take it out on me," I said, knowing Mercedes that was exactly what was going to happen because Cherry talks back to her.

"And I'm all right by the way." Cherry pulled me out of the bushes and back on the sidewalk, making it so she was the one closest to the road. "That girl really needs not to drive for the sake of life forms everywhere."

"Are you ok?" I asked, with real concern. She saved my life. Never had a friend like that before?

"Yes, if that girl stays away from the road." Cherry blew her strawberry bangs out of her face and kept one eye on the road at all times. She smelled like bubble gum from all the Blow Pop she digested. Unlike Mercedes, her name was a nickname. But she had yet to tell me her real name.

I wanted to be the one to say something to Mercedes. But I couldn't. Cursed with the ill fated toxic disease referred to as social ineptitude, I was hopeless. Okay, maybe I made the name up, but it was completely real. It trapped me into the prison of my mind, forced silent by my inability to socialize.

Except with Cherry Madison, every moment with her was a natural high, but most of all it was real, without the nervousness or the anxiety that surrounds me with everyone else my age. Radiance cascaded down from her freckled nose to her emerald Boots. She picked up a white and lavender Columbine flower and placed it between her strawberry blonde hair and left ear. Turning to me, she asked, "Does this work for me?"

I nodded. Oh, it worked for her, like everything else worked for her. Soft, adorable and funny, I couldn't ask for a better friend. She was so worth the wait. For the first time in my life, my best friend was not made out of fur or fangs and never chewed on my Carrie Underwood slippers. I hated rescuing my slippers from the family dog, Willow.

The closer we got to school, the more I slowed down. The monotony of the school year had started to bore the hell out of me. Sure, it was fantastic for the first month. Last year at my old school, I threw away my brown paper sack uneaten in the restroom trash where I had spent my entire lunch hour.

At Aspen Heights, I sat with Cherry, where we usually sneaked off campus to go to the subway behind the school's cafeteria. It was super convenient for those who hate mushy food, like me, but that and getting to sit next to her in some of my classes was the best part of my day. I was a sophomore and she was a junior, but that didn't matter that much because I was in the accelerated plus program, meaning they wanted to skip me a grade but my mom wouldn't let them, even when I transferred schools. She didn't want me missing a valuable year of high school. She thinks they're the best years of a person's life. She doesn't know me very well. That's just it. I was the reason we moved from Utah to Colorado in the first place.

I was sick of school. I wanted summer back. For now, after school was way better because nobody told us to keep our volume down or made us sit in detention in the rare times they caught us off campus for lunch, something only seniors could do. Most the time we got away with it. We were good spies.

A honk brought me back to the present. I looked over to see a car full of boys, startling me to jump about a foot. I watched as Cherry waved, while walking backwards with the Blow Pop in her mouth, where it often rested. Her tongue in a constant state of discoloration, hence, how she got her nickname, Cherry, being her favorite flavor. I still haven't managed to figure out her real name. I even tried tickling; even as she lost oxygen slowly she still never budged.

My face started to rise in temperature as I bowed my head. But Cherry didn't mind. Attention attached to Cherry like dog hair to black pants. It seemed to fit her comfortably, so unafraid and free.

Maybe the ease with the public had something to do with Cherry being from one of the wealthiest families in Aspen Heights, the only gated community. Rumor had it she used to be one of the most popular and rich ones, but she got sick of it or something and chose to be wellknown on her own terms. For some reason, popularity seemed to come with a mandate that one always had to be the offspring of parents with seven figure incomes. Most of them had chosen not to go to private school, and instead spent their money on the mile-away public school, where they tended to get special privileges because of it. The high school and the gated community were by no chance both called Aspen Shadows. Or so Cherry had passed all this information onto me during the summer.

We had become friends since I moved here at the beginning of the summer; she actually hit me with her car when I was on my bike. Not as funny as it sounds, she had broken my ankle. Since then I figured it was a lot safer for me to be in her car rather than under it. Apparently nobody around here drove very well and I fit in that way. My driver's education teacher wanted me to never drive again under his care. I'd be perfectly sane with that idea but it was a requirement to graduate.

"Life's good." Cherry brought a leaf to her nose from off a nearby blood-colored maple tree, released it into the air, and then breathed out noisily.

The air was thinner here, but I breathed easier here than my past home, a place that had never seemed home like. "Are you going to burst out in song?"

Cherry brought her eyebrows together and crinkled her nose, giving me that shut-up look.

"Sorry," I said, without a whole lot of meaning. Cherry pushed down my hat so it covered my eyes. I had recently bought the tarnish newsboy cap from Aspen Shadows Mall, by the gated community. Everywhere worth going was by that neighborhood. I guess it was in case their Porsches were in the shop or their limo drivers were ill, their shoppers could easily walk to the mall for them.

Cherry's car wasn't a Porsche, but she did drive a dusty blue Malibu. It currently sat in the shop and my bicycle wanted to stay in the garage for some much needed down time. The left tire was low and the seat was worn down to nothing.

As we approached the newly decorated vintage style school, I barely noticed the feel of my lungs squeezing inside me. My hands used to shake, my heart shivered and my legs trembled anytime I approached the school doors back home in Salt Lake City.

It was possible I had just imagined my name whispered through the crowd everywhere I turned, living in a constant nightmare. But I hadn't imagined the shoves from girls in the hallways, voices telling me the seat next to them was taken or the boys spitting on my lunch in the cafeteria.

An area code or two away, in the mile-high city, my life was completely different. My former nickname from the Satan girls, a group of five neighborhood girls who made my life a living hell, was Mousier and I hated it. Hey, no one had ever said bullies were creative. My brother had promised to keep my nickname a total secret. My old nickname could not be reincarnated into my new life. This secret had to stay in the past, where it belonged. Dead and buried.

There was another secret that got out the first week I moved to the outskirts of Denver. Cherry discovered it way too easy. Said it was obvious the first time she went out in public with me; excused me of spending too much time watching the sunbathers out on Shadow Lake and not the ones outside our gender. As much as I denied it, she refused to believe it, only said I was lying to myself. But whenever I asked her about her own sexuality, she always said she got burned in the past and was now asexual, whatever that meant.

Cherry had never told me who the guy was. I had assumed it was a guy. She had many boy vampire posters on her wall and not so many girl ones. I could never tell which sunbathers she focused on as she always seemed cautious not to stare, something I completely sucked at.

Just as Cherry and I sat in my usual seat in French class, Mercedes in a gold and green uniform, flipped around in her seat, keeping her focus on drying her freshly painted nails. "Cherry, can you please tell the new girl to stop staring. I know I'm beautiful but nobody wants a personal stalker" Mercedes pointed her middle finger right at me.

Chapter Two

I slid down in my chair, wishing I could evaporate.

Cherry sat up in her chair, placing her knuckles under her chin. "She's just trying to figure out where that wretched smell is coming from. God, close your legs woman." She said it loud enough, a few boys cracked up nearby.

I smiled apologetically at Mercedes, who grunted before turning back to her nails. I loved having Cherry watch my back and stand up for me. I only wished one of these days I could learn how to stand up for myself and use my own words to defend myself, less harsh words. But Cherry never cared what the cool cliché thought of her. She did her own thing.

I wanted the whole teenage experience, and this year I was a lot closer to being comfortable in my own skin and to having my first real romantic relationship. I was tired of just making it through the day hiding in Cherry's' shadow. I wanted. No, I needed to be able to branch out.

Maybe even become popular and a cheerleader, something I've dreamed about since my Mom started training me in gymnastics and dance on her down time, when she wasn't teaching other kids.

Today I planned to not just make it through the school day without drawing negative attention, but to talk to someone different, to make school more interesting. Summer break was sure interesting. Cherry and I both shared a love of swimming. We both swam like fishes and spent almost every waking hour over at Shadow Lake. The water wasn't warm, I mean it was Colorado, not California, but it was tolerable and fun. We did other things there too like reading each other's fortunes, playing UNO and eating. We both loved eating, although Cherry was a vegetarian.

How could I go about meeting new people? I had wanted to try for cheerleading or dance, but last year as a freshman my choices were limited and the mean girls pretty much made my life a living hell, including during tryouts. At my new school, I missed tryouts because they were last spring. I wasn't as well known as my brother, Paul, for baseball.

Having a brain never served me well socially and people seemed to resent me for it, but in this case, it served me. I could be with Cherry.

I covered my nose; the smell of my French teacher always did a number on me. Mr. Versace's nickname so fit him, smelling like the cedar and lemon Versace cologne.

Something I only recognized because he always had a bottle of it on his desk.

Quieting the last chatters of the classroom, Mr. Versace opened French class with his fluent first tongue. I only understood half of it, something about how he spent his summers studying art with his wealthy uncle and visiting the Louvre museum and then about some pyramid. I was lost, but apparently the rest of the classroom was even more clueless than me, with their puzzled expression, frantic searching for their books and scratching their heads. Some weren't even bothering to pay attention, hiding their technical devices under their desks.

That changed dramatically as cell phones dropped, heads flipped to the right and the teacher stopped his long-winded monologue. Had to be something major going on, like a fire, but all I could see was a semi-petite girl in a cheerleading uniform standing in the doorway.

As she stepped into the classroom to hand the teacher a note of some kind, the smell of fresh apples reached out to me, calling my name. She turned to face the classroom, showing a seductive smile while seeming to hide secrets behind her blood-colored lips.

The French language fell out of the black-haired beauty like it belonged to her, the language of romance.

Glued to her, I heard almost every word she said. She talked about how she enjoyed spending the last four months in Paris and all the exciting things she experienced and saw. She expressed her words harmoniously and fluently, as if she was a native.

I envied the creature in front of the class, seeming more ethereal than human. I longed more than anything to be able to talk with such ease in front of an audience. When she switched to ordinary old English, she didn't miss a beat and even in a language I could follow, she still spoke words with such romance and beauty. Sure she wasn't the prettiest girl in the world. She probably couldn't hack it as a supermodel, as she wasn't tall enough. But she made it impossible not to want her.

Hazel careened through the desks with the ease of a movie star, not floundered by the eagerness of her classmates as they acted thirsty for her attention. A few boys stood up, saying she could have their seats. But she only smiled and thanked them politely, except a boy in the second row, whom she let give her a peck on the lips. He was an attractive boy with a Colorado Rockies baseball cap. He seemed familiar. I think he was on the High School Cougar's baseball team with my older brother, even though my brother wasn't around for tryouts, they had allowed him on the team. His record back home had reached the mile-high state.

I wondered if he was her boyfriend. If he was, I so wanted to be him. If just for a day, anything to be close to her!

"That's the next-door neighborhood," Cherry said, even though I wasn't looking at her, I knew who she was referring too.

My mouth gaped open. That…was Hazel.

"The one and only," Cherry scowled and then started to remove the wrapper off of a Gum Sucker with more aggression than needed for those kind of situations. She seemed anything but pleased at the new company.

I knew better than to ask her.

Turning back to Hazel, I watched as she sat down next to the boy on one side and Mercedes on the other, who actually looked up from her nails as Hazel kissed her lightly on the mouth. Some of the boys cheered. Now I wanted to be Mercedes, only less mean.

Now I really wished that Cherry hadn't chewed out Mercedes. I clearly needed to be on Hazel's good side to make new friends around here. Cherry might not care about Mercedes or what the other GC (gated community) teens think for some reason. But they obviously had a lot of power and if I wanted to make new friends I needed them on my side.

I especially needed them on my side if I ever wanted to be close to Hazel. Just the thought of being close to her sent waves of excitement through me.

The teacher went back to his personal monologue on his summer art experiences. Wasn't sure how these boring old stories were going to help anybody understand French better. A scan through the classroom only proved they were falling on death ears.

All I could think about was Hazel. I strained my mind to remember comments Cherry had made over the summer about her. I remembered her saying Hazel went both ways. The straight side was obvious as she leaned into the baseball boy and allowed her left hand to caress his thigh.

No surprise Cherry had spent a significant amount of time talking about Hazel. Who wouldn't? Hazel was more than just pretty; she was captivating to watch and charismatic to be around. The whole class eyed Hazel and her grasp of the French language. Not sure Advanced French was the right place for her. France may be the right place for Hazel, especially with her beautiful gothic black hair, shaped in a pixie cut. She had these intense brown eyes with a sliver of hazel; it was like she could see into your soul. Her thick eyebrows and eyelashes made her eyes seem even bigger. She had pouty lips and a slightly off-center nose. Her face was completely ivory clear.

Hazel let out a high-pitched laugh that was sure to get the teacher's scorning. But shockingly no, the teacher paused briefly before going back to his personal monologue.

The only other comments I remembered coming from Cherry was that Hazel was used to getting what she wanted and she alone decided the status quo. That thought chilled me. I bet Mercedes was going to tell her all about the freak who never stopped staring. I'd be an outcast in under five minutes after this class got over.

I tried to focus on my French book, attempting to study the new vocabulary for the chapter we start this week, if the teacher ever bothered to get around to it. Before I could learn all the words, the class bell rang. I watched as Hazel got out of her seat, being careful not to be obvious while staring at her.

"You coming back to this dimension any time soon?" Cherry's words vibrated in my ear, but it took a few seconds to register.

"Present" I said, sounding more like a response to a roll call. My thoughts whirled all over the place. I decided to focus my attention on Cherry.

She pulled a Blow Pop out of her mouth, almost snagging it on one of her newly formed pigtails. Cherry changed her hair more than most people changed their mind. "Don't sound like it much."

"Well much." I was too out of it to come up with a more witty rhetoric. Getting out of my seat, I followed Cherry out of the classroom and we walked side-by-side to Psychology, another class we also had together. I secretly wished Hazel would be in the class. If so, I needed to desperately brush my hair in the girl's bathroom before class.

I excused myself to the bathroom to brush my hair and put some lip gloss on. I had a dancer's figure, tall and skinny. I wish my hair was better styled, it was stringy and long without any volume. I was awkward, still not quite sure how to handle my height. Luckily, I didn't have a pimple in sight because my skin was dry. It made me look older than fifteen, which made it easier to fit in in my classes. Not having to use the restroom, I left out the door.

Waiting for me in the classroom, sat Cherry in the back row. Trying not to be too obvious to Cherry or anyone else, I watched for glimpses of the new girl, as I sat in the back row. No such luck. Disappointed I watched my favorite class filling up without Hazel. As a few cheerleaders took the last desks remaining, there was still no sign of Hazel.

And for the rest of the morning, I didn't see her, much to my disappointment. I was so eager for lunch period that I almost jumped out of psychology class and fell on my ass.

Cherry placed her hands up in confusion as I turned into the cafeteria, instead of going straight out the door for an Italian Sub sandwich and a small fruit punch. Cherry always ordered veggie delight and hated the cafeteria. "Need something different," I explained lamely.

We walked together to the lunch line. Cherry said, "I love your eyes by the way."

"Yeah, you've mentioned that before."

"God, there just amazing."

"There just blue," I said, but my mind was elsewhere.

Cherry sighed, picking up a tray, scowling at the water remaining on the tray as she turned it around and let it drip to the floor. "Hey," Mercedes yelped from behind us.

Sure that was deliberate. I was just relieved Hazel wasn't with her.

We finished going through the food line and found our table, the one we always chose, surprisingly unoccupied, as if it waits for us when we were gone. Cherry brushed the crumbs off it, "Not sure if you forgot your sanity pills today, but this sucks. A vegetarian delight with extra provolone sounded heavenly right now. But, no we're stuck in cafeteria hell."

"Sorry," I muttered, unable to stop staring at Hazel, trying not to be a certifiable eye-stalker, but failing miserably. She sat with the other GC's, Mercedes and the boy from French class. A blonde girl with a cheer uniform, playing with her curls, approached their table and gave a squeal when she saw Hazel. She hugged a sitting down Hazel, almost tipping her chair back.

The blonde finally released her and looked my way; I immediately flipped downward to my messy hamburger, at least it was better than the green patty excuse for meat Cherry had on her plate.

I played with my food with my fork, tossing it back and forth. Finally getting the courage to place it up to my mouth, it only made it as far as my chin, the food dripping down my shirt. Damn, I had the worst aim, especially when it came to food. Also the worst timing!

I looked up to see Hazel approaching our table. I grabbed a napkin and started wiping, but the damage was already done. Her tan nose scrunched up at the food remaining on my shirt.

"Hey Blow Pop, who's the new girl?" she asked, flipping one of Cherry's pony-tails. Something Cherry hates with a passion.

I opened my mouth to answer Hazel's question, but nothing came out. Luckily, Cherry responded while swatting the air back and forth. "Kenzie meet Queen Hazel, Queen Hazel meet Kenzie. And it's just Cherry."

Hazel mouthed "whatever." Neither of them bothered to hide their mutual distaste for one another.

"And Queen Hazel works just fine for me," she smiled, as she reached in and gave me her well-manicured hand. I shook her hand, the touch electrifying me. I couldn't believe this was happening. She was touching me. This had to be a dream.

It took me a few seconds to figure out Hazel had taken away her hand, but was still gawking at me, waiting for me to say something. Anything! My heart raced, all I could do was panic.

I thought about how Cherry always says people worry more about their own appearance than about the way I sound or if I make a mistake. I opened my mouth to say something, but only dead air came out.

"Can she talk?" Hazel asked, but the words barely left her mouth before Mercedes tapped her from behind and they scooted off together, laughing and giggling.

Did that really just happen? I made the biggest fool of myself in front of the coolest girl I had ever seen in my life. The world needed to open up and swallow me down like quicksand, anything to not have to face the rest of the school day or the rest of the school year. Please say my life can go back to being boring and monotone.

Cherry inched close to me, reaching her left hand behind my back and patting me like a dog, always aware when I was troubled. We knew each other well.

"That was horrible," I whispered, not wanting anyone else to hear.

"Don't worry about it. Hazel has so many social contacts every day, she'll forget about it by tomorrow."

I highly doubted she would forget. First impressions were important, some say they're everything. And that first impression sucked. Royally sucked! I got up from my seat and tossed my excuse for food into the trash, where it fully belonged.

Tossing her empty plate in the trash can from her seat before bothering to get up, Cherry said, "Come on, if we're late, you might lose your place as the teacher's favorite." She smiled, removing her hand from my back and using it to hold mine. Something Cherry usually did to keep track of me in heavy crowds. I welcomed the comfort of her touch. It made me feel safe.

Chapter Three

The next morning, I growled when I woke up and realized my dream last night wasn't real. I wasn't cheering for my brother's baseball game, performing flawless back flips and screaming the chants right next to Hazel.

Back in reality, my ribs tightened and my stomach bubbled over. A few licks from Willow told me she'd chosen to not only wake me up but to forgo her previous suite in my Mom's bedroom. My dad and she had separate beds because he refused to sleep with the hot doggy. I could refuse but one search around the rest of my room said Mom came in sometime this morning to do some cleaning. Guess she couldn't wait in case something else living decided to show up.

A glance at my semi-clean desk, with glue on top, gave me the perfect idea to get through the weekend. I'd glue myself to the bed for two days, might not stick to my body, only a mere glue stick, but I had the whole weekend to make it work.

The searing images of the day before flooded me. Me standing speechless as Hazel stared at me, her brown eyes widening as if I was a monkey let out of its experimental cage.

Maybe Hazel's look at lunch earlier had said it all. I was an inhuman creature, but nothing of the supernatural variety like Cherry would take great pleasure in. No, I resembled more of the Marilyn Manson variety. I hated the idea of having to face Hazel again, at least not with this body or this face. Hmm, maybe there was an idea somewhere in all that.

Nah, dipping into Cherry's fantasy world was starting to mess with me. I needed to come up with some kind of way to get Hazel to change her mind about me. Nothing came to mind. It was useless.

My brother seemed to be the expert on social relations. We were as different in that respect as pretty much in any other respect.

I slowly pulled myself out of my bed, stopping to stare at the glue before heading out my door and down the tight hallway to my brother's room next door.

I started to knock on the semi-open door, when a glance at his Warriors photo reminded me Saturday was a huge practice day for him. Even when he wasn't practicing with the Eagles he was doing his own practicing.

In the picture, his goofy smile was so wide it revealed his coffee-stained teeth, My brother wasn't any better looking than I, but his personality always made up for what he lacked outwardly. He never had any problem fitting in. I knew he missed who he called his brothers, the other members on the former Salt Lake City team, but he sacrificed for me and I had to make his sacrifice worth it.

I went back into my bedroom and plopped down on my bed, enjoying the feel of the blankets beneath my back. The dog fell down beside me, trying to worm her way inside a blanket. I helped her and then reached for my dresser drawer next to my bed, where my binder rested.

I flipped through my binder from my social anxiety group this summer. There had to be some way to redeem myself in this packet, some way to get out coherent to come out of my mouth when I needed them too. My parents paid big money for this class so I needed to take advantage of it.

Searching through the worksheets, the class flew back to me. The petite girl who actually looked like a mouse and I rarely ever heard a peep out of her, but when I did it was always so complimentary to the rest of us. When she read, her voice came alive and at ease. Like all she really needed was a script to function. Two boys who seemed scared the world was going to run them over, one who never realized he was drop dead gorgeous and the other one who couldn't keep his eyes off me. They made it easy. Easy to open up and talk.

The therapist leading the group always had a grin plastered on her mouth, but she wasn't phony, she was a genuine caring person. With Cherry's help and this group, I learned there were good things about me and that I had just as many important and valid things to say as anyone else. I discovered my voice wasn't so bad after all. I just needed to find a way to bring all that I learned into my present life.

I flipped through a chapter on self-esteem, another one on how to deal with a social anxiety attack, another one on when crowds get overwhelming, but there just wasn't anything that was relevant to my current situation. The binder itself wasn't doing anything for me at this time.

After throwing my binder down on the floor, I picked up my cell phone and searched through my favorites. Cherry's picture and number were on top. I clicked it and waited for her to pick up.

Loud piano music sounded, recognizing Cherry's playing immediately. "Talk," she said, only slightly lowering the volume.

"Want to come over, when you're done, that is."

"I'm done when you get here." The beautiful music slowed to a stop, replaced by a heavy pound of the piano bench closing.

"On my way," I said, clicking the off button.

I headed out to the garage where I fixed my flat tire with adding some air but it wasn't working so I put a patch over where the air was leaking, probably someone's idea of a joke at school. I hoped it wasn't from an enemy, but so far that seemed to only include Mercedes and there were no finger nail polish on my tire so. That probably ruled her out.

After a refreshing bike ride through a few other middle-class neighborhoods the houses started to get ritzy and ritzier until the gates of Aspen Heights loomed ahead of me. I placed in the six digit code, a code that changed almost once a month. To my relief, the gates opened, and my bike adjusted form gravel to cement roads.

After a few GC houses, I saw Cherry's, large gated house, four times the size of my own, with a yard bigger than the space where our house resides. She had so many trees and chipmunks. I loved riding my bike up to her porch, as long as I avoided her Uncle. He was mean.

Speak of the devil, there he was standing there, reeking of alcohol. He saves being plastered for the weekend.

"Got a boyfriend yet?"

I shook my head no, wondering why Cherry never told him I wasn't straight. Then again, he was a racist homophobe.

"Sifting through some offers," I said, humoring him. I didn't want to be on his bad side. He's been violent to Cherry's Aunt before.

"Well it'll be one lucky man," he said, his tone creeping me out.

I knocked on the front door while he stayed in the open three-car garage, working on his Ferrari. When nobody answered, I checked my phone. The green light signaled there was a text, it read, 'Walk right in."

Like instinct, we simultaneously sat in our usual seats on the leather couch, her on the right side without a pillow and me on the left with a purple pillow she kept for me.

I wondered why, with a room like this, she drove that blue Malibu parked outside that I could see from her gigantic bay window. She explained once, said it was her mother's. But she wouldn't tell me anything else. She stayed with her Aunt and Uncle since both of her parents had passed away in an arson fire. They never caught who did it.

I mean she had a leather couch in her bedroom. Who had a leather couch in their bedroom? Who had the room for that?

Cherry wrapped me up in her arms. "So glad you're here bestie."

As always with Cherry the nervousness slowly left my body. I'm no longer drowning with shyness I got back up on the surface and started to breath easier. Unafriad to speak my mind or raise the volume of my voice. With Cherry I could be completely myself.

"So what's new, Cherry that goes on top of a sundae?" I followed Cherry's moves as she crossed her legs on the couch. Then I placed the purple pillow I was leaning against and put it on my lap.

"So what's up.?"

I gratefully picked up a half-empty water bottle left from Cherry and them I drank the rest of it in a few large gulps. Germs were never something the two of us worried about. I tried to figure out where to start, without sounding obsessed or crazy. "Remember yesterday at the end of lunch?" I didn't wait for a nod, before continuing. "When Hazel tried to talk to me and instead I made the biggest loser out of myself, standing there with my mouth gaping open. And you had to speak for me. I can't believe it. Well, I can believe it. Am I destined to live in Subway during lunch hour for the rest of the school?

"Doesn't sound that horrible? In fact, a veggie sandwich sounds delicious right now," Cherry chimed in.

My stomach responded as if it heard, grumbling loudly.

Cherry laughed and then continued to laugh. At first I felt offended, but then I laughed along with her. Her laugh was so funny and snort-like it became contagious.

Coming up for air, she explained. "You know it's weird. When I first met you, I couldn't get a word out of you, now I can't get you to shut up."

True. I closed my mouth. I do talk too much sometimes, as my brother liked to tell me often.

My brother used to be my best friend. He seemed relieved I had someone else to vent to for hours about nothing. Paul listened most of the time when his phone wasn't beeping. But his phone was always beeping. Paul never had trouble landing in the middle of the popular crowd. Here was no exception.

Cherry, on the other hand, always had to be doing something with her attention, whether watching TV or playing piano, but she always seemed to hear every word I said or pretended too.

Deciding to stop boring her with the subject of me, I changed the topic to her. "What about you?"

"What about me what?"

""You like anybody at school."

"Not really." She picked up two DVD cases from the end table next to her and then asked, "Desert Island or Blood Rose?"

Not being in the mood for soft porn and in way on overload with vampires lately, I pointed to the season one of the earlier. I wanted to keep talking, find out more about her and what to do about my problem. But I knew from experience, that Cherry wasn't the chattiest talker and you had to sometimes give her time to respond to things in her own way.

Cherry walked to her walk-in closet to put back the other TV collection. My friend was certainly unique, not that I had any other friends to compare her to. But only an interesting person would place their entertainment items like DVD collections and music CDs all over her roomy closet instead of clothes or shoes or anything that goes on the body. Rather her clothes fit inside two six-drawer dressers with scarves and hats placed on top of them. I've never seen her wear designer clothes or anything ritzy. But she did probably have every movie known to man, including probably every 3D movie that had ever come out.

A giant throw fleece blanket with the cast and crew of Blood Throat rested on her bunk bed. Only it was not really a bunk bed, because there was no bed below the top bunk, instead there rests a desk for her to do her studies, but she probably used it to spend most of her time playing on the internet. I never saw her study. She was an average student and never seemed bothered by that fact. I wondered sometimes where her drive in life was besides becoming a better piano player and memorizing her favorite teenage supernatural shows.

Cherry was interesting. She loved fun but didn't so much enjoy joining sports or joining any other kind of club or activity. She could even be popular if she wanted, possibly more popular than Hazel, but she had a clear distaste for the other GC's or for any kind of conformity.

A piece of hair flew in my face, so I uncrossed my legs and jumped off the couch to head for her full-length mirror, behind her closet door. Placing the strand back behind my ear, I stared into the mirror as Cherry approached the mirror and started making faces.

Didn't make sense that we were friends when I was somewhere between pretty and ugly, not movie star category. And Cherry easily could be the prettiest girl in school. I was a little too tall with long thin hair and a semi-flat chest. She was rounded up top in the C range and her height was something I envied, at already five-feet-eight inches tall, I'd kill to not tower over most people, particularly girls.

I bumped Cherry to get her to stop making faces and out of my mirror time. It did feel good to be able to look at myself in the mirror, something I was afraid to do most of my life, hating my reflection, but more hating the person inside it.

Closing the closet door and heading over to the couch, I plopped back down on my usual seat.

I fiddled with my crystal key necklace. The necklace was a graduation gift from Cherry for the therapy group I attended over the summer. She said the necklace was extremely valuable and that if I ever took it off, to not lose it. I wondered how some key could be so important that she wouldn't tell me why even with all my prodding and pleading.

I watched as Cherry placed the disc in the blue-ray player then picked one up one of the five remotes to start an episode of Blood Rose. I smiled, realizing how fortunate I was to have Cherry.

I tried to pay attention, but my mind was distracted from the characters in the show. I was sick of make-believe characters. I wanted a full life besides just Cherry and my family. I wanted a group of friends, like in the show, maybe even one who wanted to date me. Better yet. Date me exclusively.

I wasn't sure what I could do about my desires right now, so I focused on the show. A dorky guy trying to win the heart of a popular girl, like that was ever going to happen. Actually this sounded familiar, way to familiar.

Wait. Wait a minute.

"I'm going to do that." I said out loud.

"What?" Cherry jerked her head.

"That. The show."

"Turn into a werewolf."

Do I really have to dignify that one with a response? "I'm going to find out what she's into and pretend to be interested in the same thing." If the dorky guy can do it, so can I.

"You sure? Stiles isn't exactly the best with the ladies."

"Maybe. Maybe not. Maybe this will change things for him."

Cherry paused the show and winkled her freckled nose. "For being like brilliant, you need to check one of your fuses in the romantic department. Things are way more complicated. You can't expect a girl like Hazel to be impressed with anything other than money, fast cars and sexy people."

"No, there's more to her than that. I know it." Nobody shallow would work so hard at learning someone else's culture and their language. She seemed deep to me, even if Cherry wasn't aware of it. Maybe being too close to somebody could make it harder to see them clearly.

Sighing dramatically, Cherry swooped off the couch in one swift movement. She opened a drawer of a dresser I'd never seen her open before and came back with a stack of what looked like yearbooks and a few personal photos.

She handed them over to me, and I noticed a smiley Hazel from a few recent years. It seemed strange that Cherry had few single wallet-sized pictures of Hazel. What was she doing with those? They weren't friends before, were they? Cherry had never said anything.

"Don't ask," Cherry said, as if reading my mind.

I guess I'd have to probe her some other time. Now I needed to find out what Hazel was into, I mean besides the obvious; France, cheerleading and popularity.

Cherry took a yearbook from last year, their sophomore year, and flipped to the credits, where the students' names and every page they were on was listed in the back. Pointing at a name with her finger, I leaned in to see who it was.

Hazel Montgomery. She had lines of page numbers unlike the other students who only had a few single or double-digit numbers next to their name.

It took me almost an hour to find anything I could use. Cherry had gone back to Blood Rose.

Underneath Hazel's sophomore class presidential picture was a quote from a late nineties flick.

It appeared to be a quote from the movie. I'd heard about it, some hot lesbian scenes, but I'd never rented it. Afraid it'd be more of a porno movie then one with a plot, but it gave me an idea. A good one, I hoped. I could rent the movie and it would give me something to talk to her about. With my almost photographic memory, I'd only have to watch it a few times and be able to quote it verbatim, appearing to have watched it many times throughout my life.

"This could help. I could buy this movie and then have something to talk to her about on Monday."

"I don't know why you're wasting your time." Cherry got up off the couch and started pacing her room, avoiding my gaze.

"What, you don't think I'm good enough to be with her?" I stood up and took a hold of her arm to stop her pacing.

Cherry stood, looking past me to the window, where my memory serves to show a good shot of the side of Hazel's house. She shook her head, "Hazel would be lucky to have you in her life.

"Then what is it?"

Instead of responding to my question, she said, "if you're going to do this even with my protests, you're going to need some help, like financial goods for one." Cherry stepped over to her desk, directly underneath her bunk bed and picked up her piggy bank. She brought it over to the couch before reaching inside and retrieving a wad of hundred dollar bills rather than pennies or some other coins. My eyes seemed to bulge out of my sockets. That was a lot of money. A lot!

"I have my own money." I lifted out my pockets, but only a few quarters fell out.

Cherry half-smiled while handing over three-hundred dollar bills. I must have looked at the money as if it was poisonous because she said. "It won't bite you."

"This is too much. I was only going to buy the DVD."

"Oh, pocket change." The sad part was she probably wasn't kidding. She had three separate bank accounts, all of which she had access too. "You might need more reinforcements, like clothes, hair cut, whatever. Just take it."

"No. No way can I take this." I wasn't sure the thought of all that money made me want to vomit or steal it and run screaming, so I could pay for an Ivy League education. But stealing was never my thing. Envy, on the other hand, was my thing.

Reminding myself how lonely it would be to live alone all the time, I'd only once seen her Aunt and Uncle a few times and that was enough. The Aunt never came out of her room and her Uncle worked sixty hours a week.

Cherry protested further, until I finally gave in. What seemed like twenty minutes later and after promising her I'd pay her back. I placed it at the bottom of my country fake-leather boots, because there was no way it was going to stay in place in these flimsy pockets.

After checking her watch, Cherry jumped up from the couch and started heading for the door. I followed closely behind, wondering what she was up too.

"Work. Work. Going to be late for a very important date, no time to lose, no time to waste." She sang the entire way down the stairs and out the door. She couldn't be a professional singer, even if she bought her fans' affection.

Instead of going out the front door, she stepped into the three-car garage. Her Aunt's Mercedes and her Uncle's Corvette sat next to one another, but surprisingly she passed both of them and the key rack where both the keys rested, something her relatives must leave for her to use in emergencies.

But she passed both of them, probably not wanting to go to work in a flashy car and stopped at her Malibu, a car that had seen better days, looking way unfitting next to cars almost the same price as my house.

Unsure why Cherry bothered working as a librarian part-time, her Aunt and Uncle gave her so much money when they left on their vacations, she could create a library in her name.

"I'd ride with you home, but the books are calling." She entered a code and closed the garage before riding off into the reddish-blue sunset.

It made no sense that Cherry worked at a library or anywhere really. She was set for life. She even had a trust fund that started on her eighteenth birthday from a wealthy late grandfather.

Besides the filthy rich part, it didn't make sense she worked at a library. I mean wouldn't she be more comfortable in a movie theater or volunteering for a Halloween haunted house. I know I haven't told Cherry all my secrets, but she was clearly hiding more than I was.

Chapter Four

A glance at myself in a store window on my bike ride toward school told me Cherry had created a drastic change in me. When I brought to her the leftover money from buying Hazel's favorite DVD, Three-Way, she told me there was more I could do to impress the popular girl.

Yesterday Cherry warned me and said Hazel wasn't worth all this, as she had driven me all around in her Malibu, buying me new clothes at Aspen Heights Mall, tossing my old clothes in a dumpster outside of Foot Locker, taking me to Fantastic Sam's, dropping money as if it could regenerate itself.

My blah brown hair was no longer stringy and it blended well with the dark blonde extensions, giving me both length and color and bringing out my hazel eyes. The low v-neck Hollister top combined with my padded Victoria Secret push-up bra enhanced my breasts almost two cup sizes. While these new skinny jeans accented my bubble butt without making my hips look giant-wide. My plaid boots replaced my usual high pumps, placing me back to my regular 5'8, losing a few inches. I no longer looked like an awkward giraffe, towering over everyone, including most of the boys.

I loved my new look and how it felt, the jeans were soft and comfortable. I could now take on school, blend in, without sticking out like purple hair. I could hardly wait to get to the high school so I sped up.

The sight of a short-dark haired girl caught my attention; I was staring as she turned around, probably feeling my gaze. With a pinched expression, her eyes landed on mine. I was disappointed and relieved that she wasn't Hazel. I jerked my head away, but it was too late.

I ran into the bicycle rack, collapsing on the floor with my bike falling hard on top of me. Now I was glad I couldn't afford a mountain bike and was stuck with this small, cheap one. It still hurt, mainly from my butt landing hard on the gravel. That was going to leave one bitch of a mark. I threw the bike off me, and almost hit a freshman with it.

To make matters even worse, Hazel, the real one, passed by at that moment with the blonde-curled girl from lunch and one of my classes. I think her name was Sarah or something. Great, my whole plan today was to impress Hazel not to look like a complete freak in front of her; so far so not happening, but I did have another embarrassing moment to go on my Denver belt. Too bad a bible couldn't save me right now.

"Oh my, you ok? I saw you fall. Boy that looked bad. Should I go get the nurse?" The blonde finally stopped, standing inches from me. The sweet smell of peaches coming from her floated through me. I loved having the pretty cheerleader fall all over me. Just wish this was happening on better terms, without me releasing her hand to wipe dirt of my new butt-hugging jeans.

For the first time I noticed a few pimples outlining her pale, but pretty face. Something about this high-strung girl reminded me of Cherry, giving me the ease to speak. "I'm okay. Not a scratch on me." I lied. Sure my legs and butt were covered with scratches and bruises.

"Oh my, I'm so relieved. I hope you'll stop by the nurse's just in case. Maybe she can give you an over-the-counter pain pill. So not the benefits of the real thing, but it will help…"

Her fast words faded in the background as Hazel's huge brown eyes landed on mine, not once blinking her forever lashes, as if trying to see into my soul. I wanted to melt into a puddle and slither my way out of there. "Much better," Hazel finally said, looking me up and down in a creepy but mysterious fashion.

"Thanks," I said, wanting to say more. Wanting to mention her favorite movie, *Three-Way*, from her yearbook quote but I kind of hated it. I watched it when Cherry dropped me off last night, stayed up till one in the morning. And it was so not worth it. I preferred tragic love stories over plots where everyone was out for some big sum of money only to sacrifice all their morals to get it.

Hazel looked past me to something apparently more interesting. Not that that would be hard to do. I needed to say something. Say anything.

Before I could, Hazel tugged the girl on her arm and they headed off together. I sighed in relief and placed my shoulders back in dancer stance, straight and proud with my head up, even if it didn't match my level of confidence. Fake it till you make it, was something I heard often in my therapy group this last summer. I hate that I was in therapy, it was so embarrassing. I would melt with humiliation if Cherry, my parents or Paul ever told anybody. If Hazel ever found out, I'd switch schools, but stay in the district so my parents and brother wouldn't have to move again.

After picking up and locking my bike on the rack, I slowly moved to the front doors and into the hallway. Not ready to start my school day, I began searching for Cherry, who could always make me feel better. She had to be around here somewhere, but there were no friendly faces anywhere.

People started turning my way, causing me to worry I sported a huge stain from this morning's blueberry waffles. I looked down but saw nothing. A few boys whispered as I passed them and one of them whistled to get my attention. Certain the mockery and bullying had begun; I tugged at my extensions, almost pulling one out. I had to get out of here fast. Take a sprint and never look back.

Wait. Was that a hint of jealousy flickered in the cluster of freshman girls' faces I just passed. Something I'd only ever seen directed at other girls. I couldn't believe it. And the same boy who had whistled wasn't trying to make fun of me, he wasn't adding to it by calling me a zoo animal. He winked at me and said, "Who's the hot new girl?"

But I sat behind him in History, for a month now.

And this was only the beginning. Attention grabbed me wherever I went. At my locker, the boy next to me started talking to me. Noticing me for the first time all semester, "Hey, are you new here?"

Instead of answering him, my body froze into place, including my mouth, pasted shut by nervousness.

"Don't worry. It's always stressful you're first day. Catch up with me later for lunch or something?"

I nodded, even though I made a mental note to avoid him the rest of the day. Because of it, I packed more than just my English books in my backpack. The weight of it all made it difficult to keep up with my confident dancer stance, but to my relief the rest of the road to English was uneventful.

I stepped into English class; desperately searching for Cherry. But she was nowhere in sight so I sat down in the my usual seat in the back and opened my backpack and fiddled through it for the stuff I'd need for class, careful not to draw any more attention or get in a situation where I actually have to communicate with anyone. Especially without my backup, as sad as it is, I was terrified who I'd have to talk with next.

Don't get me wrong. I loved all this attention. I loved that people were noticing me; they even think I'm hot. It was better than a dream come true, but I was still adjusting and was worried I'd end up making an ass out of myself soon.

As more people sat down, I opened my southern antebellum novel and pretended to seriously focus on the words. Until I realized it was upside down, but fixed my mistake quickly, but not quick enough to get a curious glance from a junior gymnast, before she found her seat. I could probably teach her a few things or two, since I spent most of my fifteen years in my mom's personal gym, where she taught gymnastics and dancing. But that wasn't going to help me now. I would've tried out for the gymnastics team, but I only loved performing on the floor, hated the beams, bars and vault. They didn't have a gymnastics team here, anyway.

Plus, I can be pretty clumsy like ten minutes ago when I fell on my ass. I can't believe Hazel told me I looked much better. I assume it was a compliment. I think I look better. But what if Hazel had meant I look much better than my usual dog-ugly appearance. Maybe she just thought I passed for a human being now.

"Kenzie," Cherry called, as she skipped in side-by-side with an old-friend of hers, a senior named Sam. I wasn't sure what Sam was doing in here, advanced junior English was so not her class.

One long braid rested over Cherry's right shoulder, while a few strands of her strawberry-blonde hair fell over her left shoulder. She matched the girl-next-door type, except her confidence was way higher than the typical girl-next-door.

I waved, but Cherry didn't notice. She talked animatedly with Sam, unaware or ignoring the rude comments and dirty looks from other students. A boy in the back called Sam a dyke and a she-male.

I watched as Sam stomped over to the boys, hitting all of them with her book-bag before heading out of the classroom. The boys cowered and shut up until she left the classroom. They seemed to share my fear of Sam.

But Cherry never acted afraid. She never even seemed to care if someone was a gamer geek, a football stud, or the most popular girl in class, she treated people the same unless they messed with her best friends. Glaring at the boys in the back, she hopped into her usual seat next to me, so glad none of the teachers at this school were into assigned alphabetical seating, like my other one.

Not realizing my heart had stopped, until it started up again. I still get scared the seat next to me will never get taken, but Cherry always takes it. Unlike so many before her, she was one-of-a-kind.

"Hi y'all," I said, it was a private joke between Cherry and me. I loved using a fake southern accent, even thought the farthest south I'd ever been was New Mexico.

"Hi bloody beautiful," Cherry had chosen to adopt a London accent after her favorite vampire character of all time, from the series, she said, created the modern supernatural craze.

"Thanks hon." I told her, meaning it. I owed her in a disastrous way. Not only for the large sum of money she lent me, but for the many hours she spent yesterday driving me around in her Malibu and helping me shop and for helping me with my hair. And for even giving me the idea to do a make-over, it was perfect. Now I needed to work on my inner make-over, particularly my speechless problem I had whenever Hazel looked my way. "I'll pay it all back." I said, meaning it. Whatever was left in my savings from babysitting, allowance or from mowing my parents' lawn was going directly to her, even if it will probably only cover a small portion of the cost.

"No problemo. Jus' pocket change. What are friends for?" Cherry smiled as wide as a Cheshire cat, showing her gleaming straight teeth.

I smiled with a closed mouth, something I always did since my teeth were somewhat crooked. My parents couldn't pay for the high costs of braces. My dad wasn't insured at the time as a journalist, but now he has a good job at the Denver Chronicle with insurance. He commutes the forty-five-mile stretch everyday in his jeep. At least the paper pays for gas when he's on the job.

"Then why don't you look happier?" Cherry asked, dropping the British accent.

Before I could answer, a recording of a grandfather-clock sound interrupted us. We so didn't have one of those clocks on campus.

Ignoring the school's version of a ring, Cherry turned to my side in her chair, giving her back a stretch, while moaning in relief. "I think I broke something this morning." I could barely hear her over the chiming. She had mentioned last night she was going to help Sam move this morning before school.

I waited for the chime to end, but still with the teacher absent, loud voices drummed around the room. "Nobody put a gun to your head, or did they?" Sometimes I wondered about Sam's capabilities toward violence; seemed more on the highly plausible side. If anyone were to walk into school with a semi-automatic I'd bet it would be her. I think she's cute, dug her butch style, but every time I saw her she seemed to be physically attacking someone. Not that the other party hadn't clearly deserved it.

Why were Sam and Cherry friends, anyway? It made absolutely no equivocal sense. They were way different. Sam was a total loner and seemed to be an 'I hate the world' type. Cherry loved life and loved people, except a few popular ones and always saw the softer side of everything.

I gasped as Hazel appeared in the doorway of Advanced English. Not sure why I was so surprised, she seemed way smart yesterday in French class and she was the Junior, not me. I was the one who didn't fit in this class, that was above my class in school.

I stared entranced as Sarah and Hazel chatted animatedly, barely acknowledging the background waves and hi's coming their way.

Miss Aimee, the teacher, bounced into the room, stopping at her desk to shake her Salon-Selective-commercial hair and then approached the two royalty and they had a lengthy whispered discussion, minutes after class started.

I went back to my book and Cherry rested her head on her desk. In minutes, she'd probably be snoring so I'd have to wake her up soon. I made a mental note not to forget.

They all eventually broke up and glided to their seats. Miss Aimee positioned herself behind her desk as she started reading sections from *Beautiful Fairies*, my favorite paranormal fiction novel. The only one I ever finished all the way through.

Cherry's loud snore disrupted the reading. Miss Aimee frowned and cleared her throat, something she only did with the unpopular kids. I bumped Cherry a few times before she finally woke up, with drool dripping from her lips.

Hazel and Miss Aimee snickered. Everyone else adored Cherry. Of course they did. Cherry always took the time to listen and help others.

Miss Aimee announced we were going to watch the Beautiful Fairy movie tomorrow. I refused to cheer with the rest of the class. I liked the book more, had it practically memorized. Even though it was more Cherry's flavor of book since it was a supernatural young adult novel. I first borrowed it from her, but I fell in love with the realistic forbidden love and was never without it since. I was the one who suggested it be on our year-long reading list. Of course I told Cherry to mention it for me, still hard to talk in front of a class, unless I was reading from something. In that way, I had something in common with the shy-girl from group.

I sighed, watching Cherry pull off the wrapper of her Gum Sucker and started licking it, while taking turns to quietly hum a tune that sounded like the song she played for me on her grand piano the other day. I wanted some of her peacefulness to travel my way.

But so far peace was the farthest emotion from me. Especially when I dared look Sarah and Hazel's way, they were texting like mad bunnies not even bothering to put the phone under the desk. They were the only ones able to get away with that. It helped that Miss Aimee was their cheer coach. Sarah was the captain of the junior varsity squad and Hazel, even thought she wasn't a senior, was captain of the varsity squad.

They never looked my way, but I still worried I was the topic of their chronic texting. If it wasn't for Cherry right next to me, whispering to me occasionally between licks, I'd be locked on their every move. My nerves were so shot; I needed a licensed massage therapist or two to relax me.

When Miss Aimee asked for volunteers and nobody offered, she started acting out a scene, playing three characters. It was kind of funny. She worked hard trying to get the class involved; dissecting modern paranormal novels to read in class wasn't even a quarter of it.

I turned to Cherry, needing some sympathy and advice about my disastrous morning. I leaned over, getting close to her ear and said, "My bike fell on me this morning."

Cherry dropped her blow pop in surprise. I forgot I always told stories like my Dad with the most dramatic phrase on top. She dusted the sucker off with her hand and glanced at it, before deciding to place it back in her mouth. She was going to get thirty cavities by the time she's twenty.

I continued my story, ending with the most important part. "...Hazel said I was looking much better, whatever that means. I hope that's a good thing."

Ignoring my comment on Hazel's comment, she said "I said I would pick you up."

"I know I was there, but it's okay, you do enough for me already." I loved Cherry for wanting to help me out so much and for not wanting me to ruin my new outfit or lose one of my clip-in hair extensions. But I didn't want to owe her for the rest of my life, besides I hadn't wanted to wake up an hour early for school, since she had helped Sam move this morning from her alcoholic Dad's house to her own apartment.

Sam just got emancipated or a fancy term for becoming an official 17-year adult, and all that came with it. Didn't sound fun to me, but better than more bruises, the two of us were privy to on Shadow lake this summer the few times Sam came with us. She tried to hide them, by never swimming, but one time Cherry had talked her into it. After the heavy cover-up escaped into the lake, Sam's legs, back and arms were covered with bruises. As usual, Cherry did her best to save her, talking her into emancipation and into pressing charges against her father. His court date was coming up soon. We all hoped he fried.

Shadow Lake was Cherry and mine's favorite hangout all summer. Less than a mile from the gated community to the west rested a beautiful lake, where we spent almost all of our free time. I loved nature. Swimming in the lake was heaven, even a pleasant warm in August. The only other activity that trumpeted such pleasure was when I was dancing. So hooked to my movements, I forget to eat or take a break, something I never had to worry about at the lake because the one thing Cherry liked more than vampires was food. And she always brought plenty of it with us.

Hazel, laughing in a sinister way, brought me back to the present. I wanted to get my hands on those text messages, anything to figure out what Hazel really thinks about me. I needed to discover if I ever stood a chance in hell of becoming her friend or girlfriend, and if I ever stood a chance of making the JV cheerleading squad next year or making new friends. Not wanting to push my luck, I tried to push my romantic thoughts of her aside.

Luckily the clock chose that moment to chime. Hazel and Sarah were the first ones out as they were the last ones in. The rest of the class soon followed them, as if the last person left would somehow combust into flames.

"I wouldn't worry about what Hazel meant. I'm sure it only meant that you look hot, which you totally do," Cherry said, as we collected our things and slowly walked to our separate classes.

"See you at lunch," I told her.

"Let's meet at Subway."

When I frowned, she added. "Hey, you owe me; I cannot possibly go another day without the sweetest taste of meatballs and drippy warm cheese."

"Okay." I said, reluctant to leave my friend. We stood in front of my sophomore advanced History class, but so didn't want to go in with the roomful of strangers.

"Hey, good luck driving in driver's ed. It's your day, right?"

I grunted. "Don't remind me."

Cherry gave me a sideway hug before leaving. In the distance, I saw Hazel watching us, a shadow of black glistened in her brown eyes, as she retrieved books from her locker. I wondered what all that was about. What was it with the two of them, what happened all those years I wasn't around?

The teacher wasted no time getting me behind the wheel. Before we even left school property, I was driving. I silently hoped my affairs were all in order as he started me off with a wide street, but for the life of me I couldn't stay in the lines.

So far I had to be the craziest driver to ever come across driver's ed. Or so the boy in the backseat said as I started to run into the curb. The pig-tail girl in back started screaming. I could take the criticism, but the screaming shot my nerves.

The two boys laughed, one of them being the driver's education teacher, who was also the coach of my brother's baseball team. Paul always said what an immature fuck-ass he was. I wouldn't use such harsh words, but I agreed wholeheartedly.

I struggled to focus on the road, to keep my eyes on the white Toyota in front of me and not on the eventful day I just had. Besides my bike fall, I wanted many more of these days to come. Pretty soon I'd be a normal teenage girl who actually got invited to parties and who went out on actual dates. I couldn't wait.

"Stop" I heard two voices scream simultaneously, jerking me out of my thoughts. One seemed to come from Mr. Phillips and the other from the boy in back. Other hands took over the wheel, as I clasped my free hands to my heart; certain death was coming, at least for someone. A glance in my rearview mirror told me the pig-tailed sophomore had frozen in shock, her mouth opened and hands in front of her, without one sliver of movement. It looked like she was in one of those horror movies where all the characters freeze, at least Mercedes did. But me and the car didn't freeze and no matter how hard I slammed on the brakes, the car was determined not to stop.

This had to be bad. Afraid to look, but knowing I had no choice. I did. What I saw caused me to slam hard on the brakes, but it was too late.

I headed straight toward Mercedes and Hazel in their short gym shorts and white tank-tops. They turned around, with horror gleaming from their wide expressions as the car went at full speed their way.

The oxygen flew out of my body. I closed my eyes while pounding hard on the horn, even though I know they saw me. I wasn't thinking logically.

I started praying to a Jesus I wasn't sure I believed in. But not even Jesus could keep me from hitting the girl of my dreams and her mean side-kick, from smashing them into the sidewalk. My high-school life ruined. A knife of guilt stabbed me at my selfish thought. There could be much more at stake than a high school outcast. Like my future soul-mates' life.

Chapter Five

Opening my eyelids, I continued to pray the slow-car breaks would officially kick in any minute now. Fortunately and unfortunately the whole sidewalk of people anticipated our arrival, by the turned heads and more deaf-defying screams. Due to frantic waving from the boy from French class, wearing the same green and gold Aspen Eagles cap my brother wore, Hazel barely moved out of the way in time. I mean we landed inches from Hazel's high boots, but Mercedes was another story.

As soon as the brakes kicked in, adrenaline bounced me out of the car and over to the right side of the curb. My mouth gaped open as my heart did a double-take as a foot was trapped under the front tire. Mercedes was sprawled on the ground with her right foot captured, shaking uncontrollably. Blood covered her from head to toe.

Wait, the fear had caused my brain to play cruel jokes on me. I searched her up and down, slowly bringing myself out of shock. The frightened girl was on the floor with one foot off the curb and on the gravel, but there was no tire on top of it. No blood poured out from the large area of her skin not covered by her non-weather appropriate attire. Her arms and legs were also void of bruises or even scrapes. I couldn't figure out what had even caused her to fall. Obviously the car had never touched her.

Mercedes moved to a kneeling position, as she started praying. "Lord Jesus, thank you for not taking me so soon, thanks I can still go to second base with Mike…"

Damn, I thought this was Denver not Georgia.

The fact that everyone and maybe even Jesus could see she wasn't wearing any panties in shorts that short didn't seem to concern her. Mercedes formed an invisible cross on her busty, half-exposed chest while she made whimpering noises, sounding more like a dying bird. Guess, for a GC teen this was probably the closest she'd ever come to the white pearly gates.

Guilt slivered through me, even though this girl was not my favorite. "I'm so sorry. So sorry, I tried to stop faster. Are you okay?"

"You mean, besides you trying to kill me," Mercedes said, looking the same shallow mean-spirited girl as always. She stood up from her kneeling position and leaned into my face, so close she almost touched me. "No, you're not sorry. But you're going to be."

"Cray, Cray. She missed you by at least a foot." Hazel said, mouthing the word "drama queen" behind Mercedes back.

I couldn't believe Hazel just stood up for me. I was shocked and flattered.

"Just keep her away from me or she'll be dripping poison from her—" Hazel didn't let her finish, placing her hand over her mouth while she dragged her away. It was weird such a high-stung girl could allow herself to be controlled like that. Hazel must have some kind of witch power over people.

The teens watching my pathetic show started scattering. I wondered why everyone was leaving in such a hurry but my question was soon answered as the principal appeared. He stood there with his hands on hips, wearing a tennis shirt and white shorts, looking like he was going to cut out early.

"Go back to class, nothing to see here." Everyone else started leaving.

The last thing I wanted to be was behind the wheel again, but I was terrified the principal will scream in my ear if I didn't. As a retired Marine, he got pretty scary and ear-creakingly loud.

I got back in the car and started taking the parking brake off. The last thing I wanted to do was put it in reverse. I never wanted to drive again. I didn't have too.

Without bothering to direct me off the curb, Mr. Phillips said, "Pull out the key." Before I could he reached over and pulled it from the keyhole, causing me to jerk away from him.

I didn't want a ticket. Can anyone get a ticket without a license? I had a learner's permit. So far this just wasn't how I wanted my driving record to start and wanted to curse my parents for making me get behind one of these killing machines.

"Get out," he screamed, then lowered his voice to mutter, "I'd like to live at least until baseball seasons over"

As I started to get in the front passenger seat, he growled, "The back." He hadn't bothered to hide the irritation in his voice. "You may be the girl with the highest test scores or ECTs or whatever they are called, but you sure the worst driver I've ever had." I was sure his ACT scores were probably the lowest in the country.

That was inappropriate for a teacher to say, but he was by far more a typical run-off-the mouth coach than a high school teacher. I wanted to tell him off, but if I did I was sure to be packing for another school. He seemed to have way too much pull around here. Unless I threatened to take his star player away from him, not that was getting me somewhere. But I'd never do anything to hurt my brother, Paul.

The red-head sighed with relief as I nudged her over to the middle so she could make room for me. The principal stomped over to the driver's side window and motioned for Mr. Phillips to roll his window down.

"Fuck," he said, not even bothering to edit himself for our benefit. He took his time rolling the window down.

"Was that a swear word I hear."

"No, lieutenant. It was not," he brought his right hand up to salute him.

"If you had half a brain you would know she wasn't ready to drive yet. I hope we're not going to have to get a new driver's education teacher next year."

"I hope we're not going to have to get a new baseball coach, either." Philips said, not waiting for him to leave before he started closing the window, almost snatching one of his fingers.

I heard the principal yelp as we drove off.

Phillips had a point. He was the best high school coach in the west and his baseball team took all-state last year, according to my brother. That's why my parents didn't have to drag such a popular kid, my brother, to come here and play.

My watch told me we had another hour till the end of class, but we were heading right into the gates where the other driver education cars parked. I breathed in deeply; relieved I probably won't be driving any time soon. Just wish my parents had listened a month ago then my social status wouldn't be ruined before it even began.

Now Mercedes was sure not to allow me in Hazel's life. I was ruined. At least I still had Cherry or a bunch of mean girls teasing me all the time. It could be worse.

After school, I sprawled out on my bed, with my soft and fluffy covers over my head. I wanted to forget everything that had happened today. So far no such luck, the sight of Hazel's olive skin turning pasty-white haunted my mind. Mercedes at her side, with her demon breathe cursing me to social hell. She'd get me back if it was the last thing she did. I was sure of it. But wasn't sure what she was going to do? I shivered just thinking about it.

I had it coming. But was I strong enough to take her wrath head on. I doubted it. I chose rather to stay here forever, having my parents and brother cook me meals and hook me up with one of those catheters. In a few years, I could get my diploma from home and have a graduation ceremony by walking down the steps of my house in a square hat and a gown. But I wasn't leaving until then.

Then after I recovered, I could enroll in an Ivy League school somewhere far, far away. Maybe even out of the country.

Hazel must think I was the biggest klutz in Aspen Shadows, maybe even in the whole state. The slight progress over my makeover and the ability to use the English language or any language at all around Hazel was void. She'd stay clear of me for sure now. She may have said Mercedes was a drama queen, but she was still her close friend and popular.

Why would Hazel want me over the GC girl who seems to get everything she wants? Including a brand new fiery-red Mercedes, I guess her parents found it clever that it went with her name.

It went with her personality too.

I could hear Cherry sucking on her Blow Pop and it made me want to scream. Pushing the covers off, I grabbed her Blow Pop and almost ripped it out, but came to my senses. She was my best friend and she'd never done anything to hurt me, why take my rage out on her?

"Easy, there. It's not a bomb." She slowly tore my fingers off her stick and then placed it down on my white dresser, without bothering to place a napkin or something under it first. "So what if you tried to run Mercedes over, who hasn't? That bitch has pissed more people off than the younger George Bush."

The humiliation started to drip away, Cherry had a point. Mercedes may be popular but did anybody really like her? I wondered why Hazel was even her friend, she didn't seem afraid of her like everyone else, either. It was strange.

She tickled me under my arms, my most tick-able part, until I couldn't help but laugh. The laughter removed some of the worry from me. Things didn't seem as drastic as before. Cherry had a real talent with that. She never took anything too serious. Always the voice of reason, I wanted to be more like her.

Most of all I didn't want everyone in school to hate me by tomorrow, especially Hazel.

Cherry stopped tickling me, giving me a chance to catch my breath. "I won't let anybody be mean to you, even Mercedes. Plus, most people will probably just tell you to aim better next time."

"But I wasn't trying to hit her. I wasn't trying to hit anybody."

"I know. You wouldn't even hurt a bee if it tried to kill you. But that's you. Not me. If she wants to play some revenge game, we'll get her back three-fold."

"No, just let karma get her."

"Well, as an unbeliever in karma and the higher powers, I'm not sure I can let some make-believe force get her. We'll be gray and dead before that happens."

"I believe," I said, as a country song played in the background. The two main characters of the country movie played a musical number on their guitars.

Cherry and I met at my house after school, refusing to get behind an automobile maybe for life and I wanted to take my bike home where it was safe from the likes of Mercedes Mancini.

I had told Cherry it was either my favorite pick-me-up show or nothing at all. On normal occasions, I never picked what was playing on the TV, but this wasn't one of those normal times. Not normal at all. Hell, if only I could be normal, then maybe my life wouldn't be one disaster after another.

The wiener dog opened my slightly cracked door with her nose and came in, wagging her tail wildly. She went straight to Cherry even as I called her, jumping up and down for her attention, probably peeing on the new rug. The wiener dog turned around a few times before landing on Cherry's lap.

"We'll figure all this out later. I promise. I will keep this school the best you've ever been too. Just watch." Cherry picked up the remote, turning the volume up and placing her Blow Pop back in her mouth. "I say it's time to put our full attention on the tele. Get your mind off it. Have to admit kind of funny."

"Not to me. I don't hate them"

"Neither do I."

"Could've fooled me."

Cherry shrugged, while my Mom walked in with her famous homemade caramel popcorn. What she always makes me when I'm feeling so down.

"We're really lucky to have the best Mom ever," Cherry winked at the tall elegant woman as she popped caramel popcorn in her mouth.

"Thanks, you are my second favorite daughter," she said, before leaving the room.

She seemed to struggle saying that. I want to make my Mom happy of me. I wanted to accomplish things worthy of her admiration and respect. Sure, she loves how smart I am, but for once I want to be good at other things too.

I tossed popcorn into my mouth, the taste cream-watering my mouth. I almost forgot what conversation we were having. Almost!

But who could forget. The awful day speeded back to me and the pain I caused both Mercedes and Hazel. Not deliberately of course, at least not on any conscious level, but still I took full responsibility for it. And what do people do when they make mistakes and screw up badly. That was it. I needed to apologize. Not just because I felt guilty, but because it could be my way back into their good graces, well Hazel's anyway.

I could even give them a gift, but I had no money. Already had the check written for Cherry, with all my savings buried in it, plan to give it to her tonight before she left.

After the show was over, Cherry got up and ready to leave, with her bag around her shoulder.

"Here's this," I said, getting up from my bed, going to my dresser and collecting the check I had wrote. I handed it over.

"You know I'm just going to crumble this up, don't you?"

I sighed with relief. Even though I told her not to, I could tell she wasn't going to give in. We protested all the way to her Malibu, even while she pulled out of my driveway. But she had ripped the check up and was throwing it all over the driveway.

Back in my room, I picked up my cowgirl lighter and lit my blueberry scented candle; it caught on the first try. Highly unusual! The piece of junk was more for design purposes than practical ones. The smell would help me focus.

I turned off the widescreen television screwed into my wall, rather than the floor. My dad wanted to make my room slightly bigger than a closet and it was better anyway, now I can see the TV from my bed and not just from my yellow banana chair. The bright yellow was my Mom's idea of a funny joke. I never liked the color, but I didn't want to hurt her feelings, so I kept it.

Willow currently stared out the bay window by my bed, watching as the cars go by in the middle-class neighborhood. The two-year-old crazy dog thinks she owns the house and property, thinking it was her job to protect my parents and me.

I dug into the top drawer of my dresser; searching through pencils, folders, loose papers till finally I found my 3 by 5 index cards. Cherry wasn't the only one who used those kinds of things for non-clothing items.

I tried to write out an apology. But what words would say, "Sorry I almost killed you."

Somehow I found them. Verbal ones were always difficult to come by, even at their simplest. Written words often flew through me, as if coming from a higher power. This was no different. I believed in higher powers and karma. Just wasn't sure I believed in a God, like the bible described. He always seemed so angry. Whenever I prayed, I felt peace and love, not vengeance.

I planned to memorize every word I wrote down. So I could say it effortlessly and smoothly. I worked hard at it, even though memorization came easy to me.

Hope trickled into me as I realized this could work. These were kind, moving words and they could work. If only, I could get them to listen to me long enough or to even come near me, especially Mercedes. I'll have to pass on an apology to Hazel.

Either way, tomorrow in school, I planned to make things right with Mercedes once and for all. If I didn't, my family might have to relocate again. Also, I would never get the chance to know the girl of my dreams.

Chapter Six

At school the next day, I told Cherry I needed to go to the bathroom, where I bent over to check all the stalls for feet. I stood in front of the mirror, cleared my throat and began. "I apologize for my driving skills. I told my parents and the driver's ed. teacher to keep me from the roads, but they wouldn't listen. I hope you will find it in your heart to forgive me."

I could never be an actress, but my guilt still managed to show through the robot like memorization. Damn, I sounded like I rehearsed it a bunch of times. Well, I did but the last thing I wanted to do was sound like it. I needed Cherry's help. I left the bathroom, and went in search for her. But it was too late.

Mercedes stood in the way of Cherry's locker, while Cherry tried to push her away, but that cheerleader had some muscles. I guess all the years of Cherry snowboarding couldn't trump Mercedes inhuman witch-strength.

I took a long breath, imagining my fear leaving my body out through my mouth. A relaxation technique left over from group.

"Don't blame Cherry," I said, as both girls flipped over in surprise, stopping their shoving. I tried to ignore Mercedes below-freezing stare and focused on Cherry's loving, warm gaze, encouraging me to continue.

I started my lengthy apology or some semblance of it, anyway. "I apologize for my wild diving. I told my adults to keep me from the roads, but they wouldn't listen. I'm so sorry for the pain I caused. I hope you will find it in your head to forgive me." Okay, volume was up, but the questioning eyebrows, smirk and wrinkled nose on Mercedes face told me my words should've stayed on the page or in front of the mirror.

Mercedes probably drew the conclusion I needed to be committed to an insane asylum.

I wanted to crawl inside myself. Mercedes laughed, but finally gave Cherry her locker back and then glided down the hall to our first class of the day. I'd have to face her again in less than five minutes, according to the first clock chime. I couldn't face her again. I just couldn't. I started to run back into the restroom. Cherry stopped me.

She stopped me by giving me a bear hug, one that lasted long enough for a few whistles from boys cruising into class. "Forget about that twat. She's beneath you, just a typical insecure bully. Let me deal with her, I know a thing or two about that little witch that will keep her out of your hair for a real long time, maybe forever."

She couldn't have told me this earlier. Like twenty minutes before I made an ass out of myself.

Cherry released from our hug first, but we stayed holding hands. I studied her, as the recorded grandfather clock chimed. Once again her strawberry blonde hair was ribbon-tied up in two long ponytails and she appeared childlike and innocent. I didn't want to go anywhere today without her. Letting one hand drop, but keeping the other one, she retrieved her items from her locker and then led me down the final steps to my social death; giving me the courage to face my maker or more accurately, Mercedes and Hazel.

To my surprise, besides a half-smile from Hazel and a smirk from Mercedes, we made it to our row without any more fuss. I hated letting go of the comfort of her touch, but if we held hands anymore the class would start to wonder about us. We finally released hands, and took our seats.

Cherry smiled at me before opening her French workbook. It seemed she struggles a lot more than I do. I wished she would let me help her but she was so stubborn and independent.

Mercedes' high-pitched laugh interrupted my thoughts. I peeked at her, worried I was the cause, but Mercedes or Hazel weren't even looking my way. I followed their line of sight to Sam, standing in the doorway waving frantically at Cherry with her rainbow bracelet dangling from her wrist. She wore a holy wife-beater shirt, cargo pants and colorful Doc Marten boots.

I couldn't believe she came to school looking like a boy, at my old school it was asking to be bullied for the rest of school year. It appeared this may be the same horrible re-run and Sam and Cherry were going to take me down with them. Damn, can't I ever catch a break?

I watched as Cherry got out of her seat and followed Sam out of the room. Hope there wasn't something wrong. I worried about Sam. She had obviously been through a lot. Not only did most of the other kids seem to hate her, but her own family treated her like a pariah, worse than a pariah. They treated her as if she were a punching bag. I was never rude to her; in fact I'd only said about three words to her in the three months I've known her cause she made me nervous.

I'd follow them out the door, but I was sure Cherry would let me know if there was something I could do to help. Besides I didn't want Mercedes and Hazel to see me following them out. Things were already bad enough after almost running them over.

Currently, the two of them were huddled together and whispering. But I had no idea if it was about my mortifying apology or Sam's appearance. I decided on the later. Today I chose to be hopeful and positive, to be more like Cherry in that way. If Mercedes wasn't going to accept my apology, I was going to find a way to talk with Hazel. Instead of reciting what I had memorized, I would be simple and straightforward and take in deep breaths. I could do it. If Cherry and Sam were able to be themselves and withstand the snickering and cruel comments, I could do the same, if it came down to it. Plus, I know Cherry will always have my back.

Appearing in the class doorway, Cherry gingerly took a sip of her fruit punch Gatorade before slowly heading down her seat row. Carefree and lightly she stopped at a few desks to chat. There was no sign of Sam but the teasing wasn't over.

Mercedes called out to her, "Is your girlfriend going to join French class. I hear she could use some kissing practice."

"And how would you know? Been kissing her?" Cherry asked. Snickers from the class erupted everywhere, until Hazel quieted them down with her icy stare.

Sticking her middle finger in her mouth, Mercedes made gagging noises. But a lot less people seemed to appreciate her gesture.

It was clear if Hazel wasn't around, Mercedes wouldn't get away with being as cruel as she was. That worried me. What did Hazel see in her? I didn't get it. Hazel was kind, charismatic and complimentary to others, why did she spend so much of her time with a witch like Mercedes? Sure, Mercedes was pretty, confident and seemed like she could be a lot of fun once she dropped the mean girl persona. But she could be so vicious and unforgiving. Did Hazel only see the good in people and was therefore blind to Mercedes' cruelty?

I wanted to gag, relieved when Hazel distracted Mercedes by placing pink headphones in her ears.

"I thought I was going from a red to a blue state," I said to Cherry, as she sat down next to me.

"Not in our school, it's very much a combination state."

"I thought she was bi."

"Yea, bi not lesbian, I don't get it. They may be the chosen ones but nobody ever said they were the sane ones." Cherry twirled her forefinger around her ear, crossed her eyes and stuck her tongue out.

I laughed, even if it was kind of meanish. I guess wherever you go; people have their rules of what they will accept and what they will not accept. And Hazel and Mercedes were among the ones who seemed to make the rules.

My chest tightened as the next thought swirled in my brain. What if Cherry had told anyone I was a lesbian or Paul. They were the only two who knew. I'd have to wait to grill Paul. I checked the clock, surprised the front desk was still empty from the lack of Mr. Versace. He was more than ten minutes late. Being late wasn't usual for him, but this late could get the principal all over him. I took out my phone, checking over my shoulders to see if any people were peeking before starting my text, as usual no one paid any attention to me. 'Did u tell anyone about my, u know, preference?"

Soon after I hit send, Cherry's phone beeped. She retrieved it from her bra and began to read. Placing the phone down, she turned to me, shaking her head furiously. She closed her lips and then pretended to lock them closed.

Thank God. My secret needed to stay buried at this school. I didn't think Cherry would tell anyone, but nowadays it wasn't the biggest deal. Maybe Cherry wouldn't think that it even mattered to most people our age. Since many teens were at least bendable these days, so she said. But she could have just been trying to comfort me when I finally admitted she was right about me being a lesbian.

I made a mental note to tell Paul to keep it quiet too. I wasn't about to become another laughing stock.

Mr. Versace finally ran into the classroom, with his shirt halfway unbuttoned and an electronic cigarette falling out of his mouth. What had he been doing? He looked like a heavily drunk version of Keith Urban, sporting a few extra pounds. He could've been pretty in his young days, but wonder what happened to him. What was his story?

He buttoned up his shirt and then took a drawn-out puff on the electronic cigarette before starting his usual French-speaking monologue. Too busy concocting stories in my head about the teacher doing it with the uncomely janitor he flirts with, I almost missed Hazel yelling in French, as if we were in a stadium instead of a tiny classroom. "Pay attention." When everyone but Cherry and I seemed to understand her, she repeated it in English and pointed to the speaker in the back of the classroom.

It was weird. What was going on? Nobody ever paid attention to morning announcements, even the teacher.

I focused on the announcements just in time to hear the solution to all my problems.

"The Eagles cheer squad is in need of a new J.V. cheerleader. One recently moved away and will be unable to finish out the school year. We'll be holding practice tryouts tomorrow after school at three in the small gymnasium. Part of the work is creativity, so bring your own routine for tryouts. All classes are welcome to tryout, even sophomores. But first priority will be given to upperclassman or upper class-woman," the dorky-sounding guy snickered at his own stupid joke, before adding. "Thank you and have a great day."

"That's it." I said out loud. Loud being the most valuable word. I intended to just say that in my head, where it belonged. The girl in front of Cherry turned around to see what was going on.

"Did you smash your head?" Cherry flipped her head my way, slapping her pony-tail against the girl, who turned back around as Cherry mouthed, "Sorry."

"I want to try out for cheerleading."

"You want to what?" Cherry asked as if I'd told her I wanted to join an animal-sacrificing cult. "I want to cure cancer, but we can't always have what we want, now, can we?"

Trying to ignore her lack of support, I tried to explain, getting close to her ear. "Well, it'd get me closer to you know who?"

"What is your obsession with her, anyway?"

"She's perfect. Beautiful, charismatic, a sweetheart—"

"I get it. I get it. Personality and beauty are all in the eye of the beholder."

I ignored her snide comment. "I've always wanted to be a cheerleader, and with my gymnastics and dance experience it can't be too far of a stretch."

"Guess so." She twirled one of her pony-tails around. "Still doesn't explain why you want to subject yourself to the clone cheerleading species in this school. I personally think you'd be better off in a roomful of poisonous rattlesnakes."

I swallowed. She could be so stubborn sometimes. Why couldn't she just expand her horizons and actually try to join school teams to have memories that we can tell our kids about someday?

"Don't you want memories, be invited to the cool parties, and have more dates than you have time for?"

"I do just fine, thank you." Cherry had a point; guys asked her out almost on a daily basis. But I'd never seen her go to any of the chosen parties we hear from her house sometimes, parties happening at Sarah's or Mercedes' house down the street. And probably soon Hazel next door and I wanted so badly to be at that party, when it happens. And it will happen. I was sure of it.

Mr. Versace told the class to be quiet before he started his monologue, even though a few people still mumbled to one another. But that stopped our conversation. I didn't want to get in trouble or want any more negative attention coming at me or Cherry.

Cherry's opinion wasn't going to stop me from at least trying to get what I wanted or who I wanted. I loved Cherry and didn't want to disappoint her. She wasn't shallow and I'd love to be like her but we have such different backgrounds. There was no way Cherry could understand what it was like for me. Everywhere she looked people paid attention to her and listened to her, as if she was one of the chosen ones. Of course her income status worked for her, but nothing worked for me or seemed too.

I wished Cherry lived on the same fence as me in both cheerleading and sexual orientation. Then Cherry might begin to understand my obsession with Hazel. The most beautiful, popular and charismatic girl I've ever seen.

How could I expect Cherry to understand? From the dweebs up to the chosen ones; she was loved. She could fit in anywhere if she wanted too. I had never fit in anywhere.

Without Cherry being on board all the way this was going to be real hard. I hadn't practiced gymnastics all summer and had never once performed an actual cheer. But I danced almost every day because I loved it so much so rhythm wouldn't be a problem. And gymnastics, I hoped, wasn't something you lose too easily. I just hope I don't break my back. I needed Cherry on board, if just as a spotter. It was going to take some convincing.

From the disgusted look on her face as she watched Mercedes perform a back flip right after the clock chimed, signaling class was over. I could tell Cherry wasn't going to ever be supportive of my decision to try out for the last spot on the cheerleading team.

After she landed, Mercedes sent me stabbing eye-daggers. I had an even more serious problem. Convincing Mercedes I was worth being on her team would be the hardest thing ever. She was on JV, and even though Sarah was captain and a lot more reasonable. I know all this because of how closely I pay attention during football games, even if I can only get Cherry to stay for part of them. I needed to somehow get Mercedes to stop hating me with a passion and perfect some original cheer, with or without my best friend's help. I was about to attempt the impossible.

Cherry must have read my distraught expression because she said. "Don't worry. I'll help you, after school, my house."

I breathed a sigh of relief, until I realized it was time to apologize to Hazel. I followed her out of class and down the hallway, watching as she waved bye to Mercedes and kept moving down the hallway. I knew I'd be late for psychology but this wasn't going to be able to wait. I caught up to her, walking by her side. My lips trembled as I opened my mouth. "Hazel, can I talk with you?"

Hazel didn't seem to hear me, or was just ignoring me. I couldn't tell which. A flame of horror spread throughout my body. Was she ignoring me?

She increased her pace and left me in the dust, without even looking at me. I hoped it was the later that Hazel hadn't heard me in the first place. But of course, I assumed the worst that she hated me just as much as Mercedes. They were best friends after all.

Chapter Seven

I performed a double back handspring, landing flat on my
feet, without bumping into anything. Something that
wonderful would never happen in my room. Choosing to
practice at Cherry's house was a wonderful idea, because
her penthouse-style bedroom was massive compared to my
closet-sized room, I'd have knocked over a lamp or broke
my neck or some other appendage.

With the way things were going it wouldn't make a
whole lot of difference, anything that happened to my
body would keep me from having to face my near future.
No such luck. I was still in tact. And tomorrow I was
going to face one of the biggest turning points in my so-far
existence.

Embarrassment shimmered within me from my
vehicular mishaps yesterday and my disastrous apologies
earlier today. With each gymnastic and dance move, the
embarrassment began to diminish, but I still couldn't shake

the feeling of dread, that tomorrow could be the worst day of my life.

What if I went to tryouts tomorrow and I was so damn awful I fell flat on my face, breaking my nose while everyone laughed at me. Or what if Mercedes tripped me on purpose and I became the gossip of the school or even the gossip of Mountain Shadows. Then my family and I will have to leave town again and never look back.

The only problem this time was I had something to lose, someone to lose, that'd tear me up inside. I loved my new best friend and I wasn't about to lose her anytime soon. A lot was riding on these tryouts, but the more I thought about it the more scared I became. The clock had started to seem more like a ticking time-bomb that would explode in less than twenty-four hours.

I had no idea if it would be the entire JV and Varsity squad at tryouts tomorrow or just the coach. Or maybe just the team captains, which would consist of Sarah and Hazel. I could probably deal with that okay. But knowing my luck, the one girl who really had it in for me would be there as well. Since pretty much the three of them ruled the school.

Sure I can do a wicked back flip but it didn't mean I could do one in front of the people I wanted most to impress, including making my voice audible.

Even if it was just Miss Aimee watching me tryout, I was sure by now she knew about me almost running over Mercedes. I was screwed any way I looked at it. I had to rely fully on my physical skills and intensive training if I stood a snowballs chance in hell to make it on the team.

I needed to get a routine down pact first thing. Then maybe I could imagine everyone was in their underwear, if they were wearing underwear, pretty sure Mercedes was in the latter category. She may be somewhat hot, but I'd never touch her. Not with that horrid personality disease or whatever she's got cooking up her butt that made her snap at people the way she does. This girl has some standards. Even virgin me, who had only kissed a few girls who later claimed to be possessed by the devil or to be a temporary sinner, immediately praying during sacrament meeting to their bishop to take away their same-sex attraction or whatever those Mormons call people like me.

I'd ask my mom for help or practice in her dance studio, but I just can't tell her. She'd go into mom-mode, getting both over-excited and over-worried. I could barely handle my own over-active emotions as it was.

I was much better off at Cherry's place, although she was enthralled in *Vampire Diaries*. She just didn't have the attention span for this dimension sometimes, only for the inner world of television. But at least she's calm and rational and wasn't a Harper girl like me. We tend to over-stress just a smidge.

No matter how the day went, there was no way I was going to get some sleep without coming up with a flawless routine. Just wasn't sure what the difference was between a floor routine for gymnastics and a cheer routine. I always watched cheerleaders any chance I got, and not just because they were usually sexy, but because I wanted to be able to do what they did.

I wanted the kind of confidence it took to scream in front of a crowd, and the thrill that probably came with it. Some girls probably had nightmares about similar situations, especially if they were as shy as me, but not me. Being shy was why it appealed to me so much.

Sometimes I wish I wasn't me. I hate being the girl in the corner, or the girl in back, or the girl they walk by while snickering. I needed a break. No I needed a long break from *that* girl.

I stopped practicing, and rested my elbow on the top rung of Cherry's ladder. I looked around her room. Damn, you could fit a family of four comfortably in here. What human teenager had a fireplace in her room? Maybe those vampire characters in her TV series would. I still had a rough time putting myself in Cherry's shoes.

My room was so depressing and messy while her room looked as if it could be in the parade of homes. Her bunk bed didn't fit her decor, but there were ottomans, throw pillows and potted plants, alongside a comfortable leather couch and an impressive home theatre system.

Cherry was nice and giving, she seemed to have it all besides the most important, her parents. Everything seemed so easy for her and she was so grounded and satisfied, like she had everything she wanted. Almost everything! Spoiled rotten, yet oddly sweet, maybe it was from all the sugar.

Then again I was certain she would trade that rotten Uncle of hers and all of his money for the chance to see her parents one more time.

In so many ways, Cherry and I didn't fit. Instead of dance ribbons and gymnastics trophies, she had snowboarding awards. In place of country stars and dance ribbons, there were hot vampires and other supernatural posters.

Real life was scary enough for me, who wanted to deal with supernatural horrors? Not me!

Outside my window there was a small patch of grass before the next house while her bay window looked over the massive landscape. The yard consisted of rose bushes, a covered pool and a waterfall.

"Never going to get this done in time," I said, pulling off a back flip. That I have down. It's everything else that needed work. Especially the cheering part, my voice shakes every time I open it.

My voice shook Cherry from her hypnotic view of the TV, "Figures that witch Hazel would only give you one day to practice. You're going to burn out on the cheeriness of it all."

I half-smiled, plopping down on the floor with her and shadowing her posture, leaning on the bottom of the couch and crossing my legs. Why did she sit on the floor when there were so many comfy places to sit? I asked her one time, but the only answer she gave me was a shrug and that she felt more comfortable that way, confessing the elaborate room sometimes made her feel weird, like she didn't belong. She said she started out poorer than me. I hoped that was a compliment. I told her she could always trade with me.

"It's hopeless," I finally said.

"You could get your mom to hire a hit man so you could make the cheer team. I heard it happens."

"You got any lined up for me?"

"Yea, my cousin would do it. Just give me a fifty." Cherry clicked her tongue while forming an imaginary gun with her hands.

"I'll keep that in mind."

"Let me help you. Show me what you have so far, pretend I look like Hazel. She reached over to her collection of large Bratz dolls lining her wall and pulled over the one with black-hair, deep brown eyes, and big juicy lips and placed it in front of her face.

I laughed as she joined in. Then I collected myself and started the routine I'd come up with.

"Hmmm," I knew what that meant when Cherry did that. Something was wrong and from the look on her face she didn't want to tell me.

She played with the large Bratz doll, braiding its hair. I was always afraid to play with toys, worried the other teens would think I was immature. Cherry never seemed worried what other people thought about her, I loved that. If I could just learn how to be more like her, maybe I could make it through the cheer tomorrow.

"You're not cheering. There's no chanting or clap-slapping. Like this," she hopped up, placing her hands in fists on her side in a ready stance before she started forming letters with her name while screaming at the top of her lungs. Not that it mattered in a house this size with Cherry's Aunt or Uncle never in sight. Her Aunt's nice and all but she's always depressed and in her room three floors down. Her Uncle is always at work or screwing around with the maid.

"Go Eagles. Fight. Fight. Fight," she made fists with her hand, punching them in the air with energy and a wide grin on her face. I hated showing my crooked teeth. I closed my eyes and imagined me doing what she just did in front of a crowd minus the wide teeth-revealing grin.

"Now do it with me."

I did it with her, keeping my eyes closed. Still my voice came out only as a whisper and my peppiness probably looked more like someone in need of an energy shot. This was so never going to work out. I was screwed.

I under calculated the width of my next jump, a box dropped from the dresser floor. I stopped to retrieve the item but Cherry almost knocked me over to get it before me. "Damn, trying to injure me so I won't try out? You're getting those shifty eyes lately."

I was only teasing her, but Cherry's face dropped. Sometimes I had the worst timing ever.

Stepping a foot closer, I noticed Cherry starting to tear up. I'd never seen her cry before or come even close to it. Something important must be in that box, and not just because there was a keyhole on the outside. Maybe the same key around my neck? No, that couldn't be it, could it?

I wondered why I'd never noticed the box before, exotic wood with rosebuds carved in the top with heart-shaped brass hinges and a crystal keyhole.

Cherry stood motionless, clenching the box. I'd never seen her so still before, even when she's enthralled in her supernatural soaps.

"Are you okay?"

"Fine," she muttered.

"What's in that?

Increasing her surety and volume, she repeated without seeming to hear the latest question. "I'm fine."

Cherry seemed far away. That's good she was fine and all. Not that I was convinced in the slightest. I wanted to know what was in that box. Why did she keep so many secrets from me? Especially when I told her almost every thought that crossed my mind!

Cherry seemed so delicate, I wasn't sure I could ask her about anything right now.

I remembered her saying she had lost her real parents when she was five or six, but she wouldn't say any more than that. I thought about trying to probe her Aunt for more info, but she never seemed up to talking.

I figured Cherry would tell me when she was ready and was sure she could trust me. But we've been best friends long enough. If she can't trust me now, will she ever be able to?

"Is that about your—"

She nodded. Placing the box inside her hope chest, she closed the softly and shrugged. No wonder why I hadn't seen the box before. I'd never seen her open her hope chest before.

Cherry gave me this weird look like what was I laughing about. I can't believe I just snickered. I did that sometimes when I was really nervous. My best friend was clearly traumatized by the death of her parents and the contents of that box.

I opened my mouth to apologize, but she walked over to the radio and turned it way up, so not even a real cheerleader could shout over the noise.

She started dancing and flapping her hands like a musical seventies television show without any rhythm. She'd never make it through any of my Mom's dance classes, the others would beg for her immediate removal. Must have too much of that white-girl freckled pale blood in her, making her incapable of hearing the music correctly.

She grabbed my hands and made me join in. We banged heads for awhile and listened to some punk band from the eighties while screaming the lyrics at the top of our lungs.

When Cherry collapsed on the floor, huffing for breath, she grabbed me down with her.

The stillness brought back my worried thoughts. How could I ever make a squad if I couldn't even project my voice to my own best friend? It was even hard to bang my head around her and act silly. I always worried what people thought about me, even my own best friend.

"What am I going to do?" I finally said out loud, barely realizing it.

"Practice screaming in a pillow or in your bedroom when you get home, until you feel more at ease with your voice and then tomorrow morning we can go over to Aspen Heights park and practice or something."

All those seemed like good ideas so I nodded, a rock full of tension leaving my body. What would I ever do without Cherry? She was such a lifesaver.

"Are you sure you want to be a cheerleader? You haven't heard about what happened to the last cheerleader?" Cherry said, in a deep dramatic tone of voice. "You don't want to end up like the last cheerleader; she went to a tea party and never came back."

"Why, what does that mean the last cheerleader? Was she eaten by zombies?"

"Just her brain, that was before she fell into a rabbit hole."

"You're crazy," I told her.

She nodded.

"So what happened?" I asked, failing to hide the eagerness in my voice.

"Hazel got to her, do I need to explain further?"

"Now if you had said Mercedes. No."

My phone buzzing interrupted the conversation. I looked down to see who it was, intending to ignore it in case it wasn't important. But it was my Mom and it was past eleven o'clock. I'd get the fifth degree if I didn't answer. Cherry was lucky she could stay out all night if she wanted and nobody would notice. Then again that was kind of sad,

"Mom."

"Come home now."

There was no arguing with her. And there was no time to try to figure out what Cherry's deal with Hazel was. I'd have to figure that out for a different time. And I needed to find out what happened to her real parents.

I waved to Cherry and left her room. I went out the back door where my shabby out-of-place bike rested on the brick wall. Before getting back on my bicycle, I turned around and waved at Cherry.

She waved back, watching me from her window while twisting her crystal key necklace around, then placing it back under her shirt. Cherry was just one big mystery that I couldn't quite solve right now.

Because I needed to figure out a way to perform a full lobotomy on my personality by tomorrow, if that started with screaming in my pillow. I had to start somewhere.

Chapter Eight

The closer tryouts came, the more time stood still. The back seat of the old Ford Taurus was only making me feel more anxious and eager to get them over with. I was so ready for it. Either I was going to stick the routine down or I was going to just look like a loser. But the waiting was killing me most of all. Every one of my nerves was fried. All throughout school and in my nightmares last night; evil butterflies tortured my stomach. I was about to throw up dark butterfly wings everywhere.

All the screaming in my pillow and Cherry's cheer tutorial wasn't going to help at all if I couldn't come up with the voice to go with it. I'd end up having to spell out letters with my body instead of my voice. But that wasn't what real cheerleaders did. They yell loudly and try to get the crowd all riled up. I was worried I would never be peppy enough. I guess I will never know unless I try.

I may have had the routine flawless, but that was this morning in front of my mirror. This wasn't going to be anything like my mirror. This was going to be the real thing, topped off with possible harsh criticisms and judgment. Then again I could nail it. Anything was possible. I needed to let Cherry's positivity rub off on me. Maybe if I started sucking on a blow pop,

It was going to be a lot different in the gym with people who potentially hated me. If Mercedes was there, I didn't have a prayer. There was no question she hated me with a passion because I almost ran her over. Even though I didn't give her a scratch, she was kind of mean. It wasn't fair that she was one of Hazel's closest friends. But life wasn't fair.

I just needed to focus. Focus on the moves I worked so hard at perfecting. I ended up saving the gymnastics moves for the end of the routine and emphasized my dancing skills whenever I could between chanting, "Go Eagles. Go. Fight. Win." Not very creative I suppose, but it was better than no chanting at all.

All throughout driver's education as the moments ticked on.

Even thought they tried to throw me off by giving me the wrong day, I made it barely to cheerleading tryouts.

It was during ninth grade tryouts. I was such a fool to believe my back flip was going to get me on the team. Sure it seemed to impress the former cheer squad, who all looked at me with awe. That was until the chanting started, my voice betrayed me. It didn't help that the six girls who made my life miserable were there in the stands, cat-calling, being bitchy, and laughing. I ran off the stage before I could finish.

Was I doomed to have the same experience in tenth grade? Should I wait another year, practice some more, try to learn how to be more confident. Would that even happen? Or would I just be more of a coward next year and just chicken out entirely. Was it now or never?

I wasn't going to find out. If I didn't face my fears now, I'd never face them.

An obnoxious noise brought me out of my thoughts and back to the moment. "There is such a thing as a gas pedal," the boy in back said to the redheaded girl as she slowly turned the corner of the Taurus.

So glad I wasn't driving today, I would've killed everyone in the car by now. My patience wore thin as the redhead drove super slow back to the school. According to my wristwatch, the final bell was minutes from ringing and we were about three or four miles away from the school. If I were to hop out of the car and take a run for it, I'd make it back before this sixteen-year-old grandma did.

I wanted to slug this tool next to me, who kept scooting closer and closer, ever since my new look he never stopped hitting on me. Besides he smelled like gym socks and blue cheese, with a little bit of Axe body spray.

"Not interested." I said, for the thousandth time. He was a total ass before, especially when I drove. Now he just won't leave me alone.

When we finally arrived at the school, I jumped out of the moving car. But I still couldn't dodge the blue-cheese smelling Brad. He could be cute if I was straight or if he took a shower once in a while. "Don't want to sound mean, but you're not my type."

"I'm every girl's type."

I jerked around him, just in time to escape a hug. "I'm not every girl."

Leaving him behind, I hurried into the building. I hated rejecting people, but he was probably used to it, and it wasn't like I could tell him the real reason. that I just found him physically undesirable.

When I reached my locker, Cherry was there, pulling out a red blow pop. "You want me to come support you?"

"No," I said, my words sounding harsher than I intended.

She stepped back and her mouth opened, giving me an 'You just stepped on my toe,' look.

I threw my school backpack in my locker and collected my gym bag. I needed to go change fast and get to the gym, I couldn't let Cherry hold me back. I opened my mouth to explain, hoping she'll understand in a timely fashion. "Sorry, I'm too nervous. If you were there, I mean I'd love to have you there, but I—"

"Say no more," she interrupted, placing her hands up. "I get it. Call me when you're done and kiddo, break a leg."

That was a definite possibility.

I looked around the waiting room, not even sure how I got down here, I was so nervous. I held a number in my hand. It said ten so I assumed I wasn't up for awhile since they just took in number one. Most of the fifteen or so girls in the waiting room looked familiar, but I didn't know any of them personally.

Obviously the girl next to me noticed my nerves and said with pity in her blue eyes, "Maybe if you get it over with, you'll feel better. You can take my number."

I nodded, relieved to be now holding number two instead of ten.

Sarah poked her head into the room. The girl who gave me her number pointed at me, signaling it was my turn. My lungs seemed to fill with water, till I couldn't breathe. Need air quick.

My legs were like rubber. I couldn't move them.

Sarah reached for my hand, a warm friendly gesture, especially from someone I barely knew. "Oh my girl. You're shaking. Don't worry. I'll be in there the whole time helping you through it. Just imagine the four of us are in our underwear or something equally horrendous."

That would not be anywhere near horrendous, but I had no voice to argue with her.

Sarah released my hand as we went into the small gym, a large floor mat and three girls waited for me, sitting behind a foldable card table and on top of plastic chairs. Miss Aimee stood against the wall, allowing the girls to take over.

Too scared to look at the one in the middle I've crushed on ever since I first saw her glide into the room like a beauty queen. Lucky Sarah, who sat on her right, smiled and winked at me, saying in a perky tone, "Hello Kenzie, we want you to start whenever you feel ready."

I started my moves but my shaky voice betrayed me, revealing my lack of confidence. I watched as Mercedes sat between Hazel and Sarah, seemingly way busier with nail polish than in what I was doing. That brought me back to summer group therapy and what the therapist said often, 'Most people are way more worried about themselves and how they look then they are of you.'

I took in a deep breath before starting over.

"Go. Fight. Win," I said, in a stronger voice.

I performed the moves as best I could, but I kept forgetting a few steps here and there, a few hours yesterday and a few at home last night wasn't enough for me to memorize a routine, at least not performance ready. And it showed. Even worse, I couldn't even hear my own voice as the music stopped and I had started chanting.

Then nail-focused Mercedes brought her head up, grinning at my disaster. That alone would haunt me for a long time. I would have run out of the gym right there, but my legs were frozen shut from the fear.

Hazel sighed loudly, getting up from the middle of the table. Sarah exchanged an 'I'll handle this' glance at Hazel, who responded by placing her knee on the chair, ready in case she was needed.

"Oh my Kenzie you're brilliant, just need to work on your self-esteem some. Let me help."

"This is a waste of time," Mercedes said, flipping her hair.

Sarah continued, ignoring her. "Ever sang in church?"

Why was Sarah asking about Church? Did she know where I came from? This wasn't exactly a small town, or even that small of a suburb, there was no way she would know. Would she? Was I just being paranoid? I didn't want anyone knowing I came from Mormon city.

Picking up a clue that I wasn't going to respond anytime soon, Sarah answered for me, "I'll take that as a no. Hon, we need you to project from the diaphragm." She placed her right hand on her stomach below her breasts and another one on her chest. Make sure you are yelling from this part not this part. "Don't be afraid, just pretend you are in the shower and nobody is listening."

Trying to ignore Mercedes staring at me as if I was a science experiment gone wrong, I did as she said. Some more volume came out, but not enough to be impressive.

"Much better! Work on that, m-kay. Awesome moves." Sarah smiled.

"Thanks for your time," Hazel said, watching me closely with those humungous brown eyes of hers that seemed to probe inside my very soul. I knew at that moment that there wasn't going to be any dream wedding for me and Hazel and definitely no cheering in front of a stadium full of people.

I never really thought about the being in front of an auditorium full of people, always just considered the being popular and pretty in a short skirt thing and being able to do cool movies and dance.

The comment translated to me as my cue to take a hike. I collected the bag of bones that felt like my body and wanted to move faster, but my legs were a watery, sweaty mess.

"We can cross her and her little mousy voice off." Mercedes said.

"Not so fast. You're just bitter because she almost ran you over. At least someone had the guts to do what everyone else in school wanted to at least one point in their high school careers." I overheard Sarah's voice before the door closed behind me.

I fought the tears wanting to escape, even though it's more likely an asteroid will fall and destroy the Earth than if I made JV cheerleader, things could always be worse. I still had my best friend and a supportive family.

Damn, I was such a fool. I ran out the back doors of school as if a pack of werewolves were chasing me. I couldn't even look back at the real-life nightmare.

Chapter Nine

I can't believe I just made a fool of myself. I had ruined my dreams of cheerleading and Hazel.

I managed to remain semi-invisible for a month now and hardly anyone picked on me at all. If they tried, Cherry glared them down with her laser-like eyes, the perfect bodyguard. I can't believe I put that in jeopardy. Would Cherry even speak to me if Mercedes and the other cheerleaders started to bully me? Would she speak to me when most of the school joined in, since Hazel seemed to make the rules in school?

Humiliation covered me from head to toe, as I headed straight home in my Mom's car, with my bike barely fitting in the back of her minivan. I called her because I didn't think I could ride my bike home without crashing into something or someone. On normal circumstances I struggled with staying in the bike lanes or on the sidewalk. Hitting the occasional side tree was quasi-normal for me.

My mom looked out her side window as we drove past the gates of Aspen Heights, probably trying to relive her glory days. She grew up in one of the richest neighborhoods in Utah and was on both the dance and cheer teams in high school. Probably disappointed she ended up with a daughter who couldn't cut it socially or follow in her footsteps when she worked so hard with me growing up, allowing personal time to train me. I worked better without the others around. Always alone! With the way things were going that wasn't going to change.

She turned to me, concern in her voice. Guilt dripped inside me like the water bottle I jugged.

My mom was more like Cherry, kind to everyone, no matter what their station in life. She wanted others to be happy, even before herself. "Oh honey. I wish you would've told me you were trying out. I could've helped you. I'm so sorry."

Her high-pitched words weren't helping. My Mom meant well. She always did. My already shot nerves just couldn't take it.

"Not your fault. None of this is your fault." I turned up the radio, but she tried to speak over it and I shook my head, signaling I couldn't hear her.

"Mackenzie April Harper," she screamed.

I can take a hint. I turned the radio down and listened.

"Tell me how I can help you?"

"You can't. Nobody can." I mumbled, meaning every word. I was hopeless. There was just no way around it, particularly in the social department.

Sighing, my Mom turned the radio up a few notches, finally leaving me alone to my own misery.

My mom wasn't my first choice, but she had a break between dance classes so it was easiest for her. I had called Cherry and Paul, but one was working at the library and the other one was at practice, even if baseball season was in the spring, they practiced all year long. They both ended on the note they would come find me and check on me as soon as they could. It helped knowing people cared about me.

I appreciated all their concern, but right now I just wanted to be alone. My Mom wasn't getting the hint. After we reached the house, she followed me up to my room and sat by me on the bed.

I crawled under the covers, including my head, hoping she'd take a hint. That word must've skipped her generation.

I tried to ignore the embarrassment spreading throughout my body, and my Mom's panicky voice going on next to me. "If we have to we'll find another school for you, we will."

She wasn't helping. I didn't want to find another school. I needed to learn how to stick it out. Even if the bullying started up again, would Cherry be able to take it with me? I assumed she could, but so far almost everyone I was semi-close to outside my family had let me down at one point or another?

But Cherry was different. For one thing I couldn't begin to imagine what it would be like losing her. I don't think I could deal with the rude comments and snotty glares.

I doubted Cherry and I could stop the bullying if it got out of control. Paul or I couldn't at the last school, but here's hoping and praying. Maybe! Just maybe this school in Colorado had more class than the one back in Utah. Maybe having an unrelated best friend would make all the difference.

My Mom must've gotten the hint, because I heard the door close. A few seconds later, it reopened and I heard her voice, calmer this time, as if defeated. "I'll make your favorite, caramel popcorn, and it'll be ready when you're done taking a nap."

"Thanks, Mom." I wanted to tell her I appreciated her, and I was sorry for being rude. But I didn't have the guts.

All of this, including stressing out my Mom, was because I wanted to prove to Hazel I was more than just the quiet book-wormy type. I can be sexy, I can be adventurous and there was more to me than the girl who couldn't drive.

I can't believe I thought I stood a chance of making the team, especially with Mercedes and her threats to make my life a living nightmare. It hadn't mattered that I had years of gymnastics and dance training, before. Why would it matter now?

What seemed like hours later? I could smell Paul seconds before he attempted to lift the bedspread off my body, the scent of his hot sweat and wild sunflowers almost made me vomit. I fought him every step of the way, but he was strong. All the weight-lifting sessions he was required to do for baseball clearly worke.

I growled, when he had me completely bedspread free and wouldn't give it back to me. I reached for it, but he tossed it out into the doorway. I almost slammed him on my way to get the blanket, but he blocked me before I could, strong enough to pick my ass off the floor.

"Put. Me. Down." I told him, "or I'll tell Mom about your playboy stash under your bed." I know because he shared them with me. He never seemed to mind having a sister who's gay, even though it took years for our parents to adjust.

He placed me on my bed, a bit roughly for my taste. So I grabbed his arms and coaxed him to sit next to me. He did, placing his hands underneath his chin. "So what's wrong my favorite sis? And it's not just because you're my only sis, you know it's really true."

I half-smiled.

He playfully touched the side of my lip to make it a full smile. "Much better."

"How was practice?"

"The greatest," he said, with a wide-tooth grin. He never worried about showing his teeth and why would he? He was born with straight, cavity-free teeth.

It was great to see him so happy, especially since he had to leave so many friends and even a girlfriend behind. They still chat on webcam but I can tell sometimes he misses her and their relationship was struggling with the distance.

Gratefully baseball at Aspen Heights was huge, that was one of the reasons we located here, and the coach, hearing about Paul, let him on the team without even a tryout. Plus it was only a forty-minute commute to my Dad's new job as a sports writer for the Denver Post.

When I didn't respond, he said, "Do you need your big brother to step in, rearrange some cheerleaders for you."

"Yea, Mercedes." I joked, even though a part of me wished he could do just that.

"I'll have a talk with her, before you know it she'll be begging to do your homework."

"That would be bad."

"Me talking to her or her doing your homework?"

"Probably both."

He twisted his Colorado Rockies cap backwards as I reached for my Febreze bottle and started spraying him. He lifted up his right arm, sticking out his armpits so I sprayed there and then he did it with the other arm. He was so funny.

I wish I could be him for just a day. All the cool, social genes went to him and there was next to nothing left for me. He struggled with academics though, so it was good he was rumored to be their star pitcher this season. He could get an athletic scholarship, if he chose to accept one. He was a junior and probably hated the fact that most of my classes weren't open to him because of his lower test scores. But still I'd trade all that in to be the socially gifted one. Life always seemed so easy for him, girls, sports and my parents' admiration. They never had to rescue him the way they did me.

The clacking of Cherry's high pumps interrupted us. I looked up to see Willow jumping to her knees, she bent down to retrieve the whiny dog, who might've given her a splash. Sure hope not. That was why my Dad had to remove the carpet from my bedroom and put in hardware floors at our last house. This time he made sure there were only a few rooms with carpet and those stayed doggy-free.

Paul grinned again at the sight of Cherry, something he always did. He hopped off and gave her a friendly hug. I wanted to remind him that she was my friend, not his. But who was I kidding? The only friends I thought I had only came over to see him. Except Cherry was different, she didn't hop up and leave with some flimsy excuse every time Paul left or wasn't home. I was so lucky to have her. To have all of them!

"Someone's been hitting the cologne mighty hard this evening," Cherry said, as she scrunched up the freckles on her nose at the scent.

Willow came to rest on my lap, as I placed my back against my headboard. Cherry sat on the bed next to me, unusual for her, as she loves the floor in my place. She rested her backpack on top of her crossed legs.

Paul sat on my other side. They both simultaneously placed their arms around to my back, as if in total sync. The two of them together were so entertaining and funny; they had a similar sense of humor. I was so lucky I had all three of my best friends here in one place, with one of them trying to decide who she'd rather sit on, as she tickled my legs with her long nails and the other two making funny faces every time I looked at one of them.

Why was I about to cry when this moment was so perfect?

I never cried, anymore. That was the old me. I got sick of crying myself to sleep every night in the fifth grade. My mom helped me and found a better, supportive teacher for me in the sixth grade and from then on I promised not to cry. I owed it to my Mom to learn to control my emotions better and that nobody was worth crying over. I developed a hard shell and I just needed to figure out a way to tap into it again.

Cherry noticed my sad face, as she stopped and focused on me. "Hey, it's not as bad as you think. It never is."

"It's not?" I asked, my meek voice such a contrast to her confident one.

"It never is," Paul chimed in.

It was easy for both of them to say. They never had a problem speaking their mind or doing what they wanted to do. I loved dancing and gymnastics more than anything, but we had neither of those teams at Aspen Heights. Probably because their main focus was on baseball and football. It sucked royally.

"You're confidence doesn't seem to match what you're able to do and who you are. Hey so what if you don't become a cliché cheerleader? Who cares? You're beautiful, smart, and a fancy gymnast dancer," Cherry said.

"What's a gymnast dancer?"

"You. You're special and unique. That's why we love you."

"Special?" I asked, unsure if that was an insult tor a compliment

"Yes, special, in a good way." Cherry took my left hand and started rubbing, sending chills up my arm. "You don't need to drop a few IQ points and flick flimsy pom poms around, exposing panties every time you jump, like some stripper."

"Yum panties. Not sister panties of course. Ick," Paul said.

Cherry opened my top drawer without even looking behind her and threw a pair of socks at my brother, probably assuming them to be panties. He began putting them on his feet for God knows what reason.

"Cheerleading is so passé anyway. This is the emo world. If you want to be cool, you get the black eyeliner." Cherry reached inside her Betty Boop backpack and handed Paul some eyeliner, with one sock on, he began placing it under his eyes.

I snickered, unable to laugh. It still hurt to breathe, but I loved them for trying so hard to make me feel better. And I did feel better. I wished I could stay in this bedroom for the rest of high school and never have to go back.

"Plus there's always next year, you're the best dance gymnast I know."

"Gymnast dancer," Paul corrected her.

"Huh? Spaghetti Spaghettis same diff," Cherry said, such the sister I always wanted, fitting so well in our three musketeer thing.. What would I do without her? Without any of them?

Paul shook his head and rolled his finger around his ear, signaling she was nuts.

Cherry answered by throwing one of my decorated pillows at him, before hopping off the bed. Where she started performing what could be passed for a cheer routine. Maybe. Her arms and legs weren't straight, her chanting was almost too loud and her jumps barely made it off the floor.

Paul joined in, making it even worse by almost breaking my desk lamp. This time I laughed and couldn't stop. Like a ton of bricks being lifted off my chest. When he tried to do the splits, it sounded like he actually did break something because I believe I heard something rip. And that was not an inanimate object.

Paul nursed his wounds, holding his balls while Cherry gave up on her own comic cheering and plugged her music device in.

Cherry danced like an overly-caffeinated zombie. Pretty soon Paul joined in, moving as if he was on crack, jumping up and down while banging his head side to side. The song didn't call for such extreme movements.

Cherry pulled me off the bed, trying to convince me to join in. But when I did I felt stiff and self-conscious. I couldn't relax the way they could.

Another glance at both of them, looking to be in mid-seizure, helped me some. Someone had to show them how it was done. At least I had some semblance of rhythm so I started to do one of the dance routines I still had memorized. Cherry and Paul tried to join in, completely messing it up. I laughed so hard I couldn't dance, either. Pretty soon we were all rolling on the floor, with uncontrollable fits.

The laugh ended with a shared stare between Paul and Cherry, looking way too long to be platonically based. Was Cherry going to become my sister for real some day? I ignored the tug of jealousy in my gut, chalking the feelings up to the knowledge that may never happen to me. I may never get anyone looking at me that way.

Especially since I only liked girls and besides Cherry, I've never even gotten to know one before. Never even been on an official date, only kissed a few girls from other schools that I met at dance camps, but they always pretended nothing had happened; then made it clear to everyone, as if their Mormon bishops were listening, that they only liked boys. One went so far as to make-out with my brother right in front of me. Guess to prove to me she was straight. All she proved to me was that I could throw up without having any physical cause.

Cherry abruptly stood up, checking her phone messages. "I need to get home," she said, hugging me from off the floor before leaving my room in a strange fashion. Willow and Paul followed her out of the room, like lost puppy dogs. That was probably the last I'd see of both of them tonight.

I jumped over to my blinds and opened them up, searching for Cherry and Paul, worried they were going to share a goodnight kiss. I know he liked her, but she'd only ever shrugged and responded with a 'Not my type.' Totally confused me since Paul seemed to be everyone's type and their chemistry and personalities meshed together so well. Why was Cherry so anti-relationship anyway? Even a legally blind person could see the sparks flying between the two of them.

I watched as the two of them came out the front door. Paul walking her all the way to the driver's side of her Malibu, she gave him a half-hug before hopping into her car. That hug looked nothing close to romance. I wasn't disappointed though, I wanted my best friend to myself.

The alarm clock flashing interrupted my thoughts, as it does every time on the hour; most of the time I never notice it. I couldn't believe it was already eleven. The last few hours had flown by with no French homework done. Damn. Have to set my alarm for early tomorrow because study brain time was way over.

But I needed to focus on my social dilemmas before bed, like how I was going to face Hazel, Mercedes and Sarah tomorrow.

Maybe Cherry and Paul were right. There was nothing wrong with me. The only thing seriously wrong with me was the way I perceived me and the way I acted because I thought I was nothing. Well, Cherry was usually right and if she believed I was smart, beautiful and talented, maybe I was.

If I act like the tryout was no big deal. So what if I didn't yell loud enough? I had managed to perform the routine almost flawlessly otherwise, including a front twist and back flip that some of the Varsity cheerleaders probably can't do.

Maybe there was a way to redeem myself and things weren't as bad as I thought. I went over the rest of tryouts in my head, like a horror movie, trying to get some distance to think objectively. It sort of worked. All I could come up with to redeem myself was maybe to become friends with the nicest one, Sarah. I was friends with Cherry and she was a junior. It was possible Sarah would be my friend. She seemed to be genuinely rooting for me and standing up for me against Mercedes, when she thought I couldn't hear her.

I could practice for a year and try again next year, when my courage matched what I was able to do.

First I could work on Sarah, trying to get her to be my friend. Can't be the craziest idea I've ever had. Or could it? Could popular people like Sarah really see anything in me worth getting to know?

Not like I'd be using Sarah. I wanted to get to know her, she seemed nice. I believed she was straight like Cherry, but that only made it easier. I could have two best friends instead of one. Life was looking up already.

I released the curtains, as they flew back in place, deciding the best place to start was with social media. I retrieved my purple laptop from my desk table and typed into a Colorado social network site, where I searched for Sarah's name. Barely remembering her last name from class, I knew it started with an R. There it came up. Sarah Ryan since Cherry was our mutual friend. I hadn't known they were friends at all.

I sent her a friend request, hoping she wouldn't mind. Maybe she'll even want to be my friend too. Either that or I've managed to plunge myself deeper in the social hole. Time will only tell.

Chapter Ten

Checking my mile high chat account for about the thirteenth time, I wasn't watching where I was going so I bumped into someone. Knowing my luck, it didn't surprise me when a pissed off Mercedes turned around with a glob of pumpkin latte spilled all over her fancy studded shirt. Her devilish smirk and wicked green eyes flared. "Next time this is going to be your brains spilling down my three-hundred dollar Prada shirt."

"Sorry," I mumbled, but it did nothing to stop the steam seeming to come from her ears. My goal was to befriend Sarah and so far nothing had happened there, not even a friend acceptance on chat.

But I did perfectly reach my opposite goal of pissing Mercedes off more. I was probably already the first on her death list as it was. She could be the next Supergirl. Her laser-like glare that seemed to have the ability to penetrate right through me, telling me my death might be even closer than I presumed.

Luckily, someone came to keep her from pulling out a hidden switchblade or gun. Not that anyone could get those kinds of things past the high level security metal detectors this school had to offer. But Mercedes was a GC and her parents could be paying for the whole security system, so who knew?

"Relax, Mercy. Take another valium." Hazel said, approaching from behind, looking like a character in one of Cherry's vampire shows; with an air of breathtaking charm. I wished she'd lean in and suck my blood, anything to feel her body close to mine.

To my disbelief, she smiled at me. I wondered if I hadn't woken up yet.

Mercedes sneered like a Pomeranian, ready to attack. "Or I could just take Kenny, is it, and ream her—"

Hazel placed her body in front of Mercedes, pushing her out of the way and then turning around to face her friend. "I'll take it to my dry cleaners, on me, they're the best in the state."

"Nice and all but what do I do in the meantime and what do I do about my half-empty latte."

"Not your assistant. But there's a Hollister top I left in our locker, in my gym bag."

"Better not be smelly," she said more to me than Hazel, and walked out of the French classroom. Even though the final bell rang, there was no sign or scent of Mr. Versace. I went to take my seat, disappointed Cherry wasn't there yet. She usually made it before me since she had the convenience of an automobile.

Hazel whispered something to the boy in the seat in front of me, who later moved, allowing her to sit there, something she had never done. I almost passed out. Her usual seat was on the other side of Mercedes, who sat kiddy-corner to me.

"Was just going to tell you that your gymnastics and dance moves are perfect for Junior Varsity, but the cheering could use a lot of work." Hazel took a few steps my way, causing my legs to almost collapse into jelly. So mesmerized by her I couldn't remember what she had said.

Too much time passed than what's normal in human conversation. Luckily, Hazel filled in the void. I didn't trust my voice to betray me.

"You ok?" she asked, crinkling up her nose, probably wondering if I was stoned. That sparked a memory of Cherry saying Hazel and her friends loved to do that often. Something I'd never done or would want to do. But never say never.

I couldn't stop staring at her, motionless. I finally nodded, while trying to picture my brother's face on Hazel's. Oh that body was so incredible. Late stages of a B cup and smooth soft legs, imagine Paul's hairy legs. Ewe. Say something. Anything. Just to get words out, or even just sounds. "O…K.." I said, as if I had a serious stuttering problem. Damn, real smooth.

I heard a thump on the seat next to me. Before I turned to my right side, I knew who it was. Cherry blew a large bubble, eventually letting it plop and splatter all over her face.

Hazel rolled her eyes at Cherry, who only smiled and tilted her head in response. "A—right. Jus be ready at five, your place," she twirled around, but not in a high energy Cherry fashion.

Hazel moved with a crafty style and sexiness like the jaguar tattoo on her lower back probably would, but it wasn't an average tramp stamp. Nothing on her seemed average or trampy. I'd never seen her tattoo before, but being right in front of me wearing a blood red shirt that had to be extra-small, made it easy to stare. Easy to notice the softness of her silky black hair and the tan-color of her lower back. Cherry and I had swam and laid out most of the summer at Shadow lake and we weren't close to as tan as that. Well, maybe I was, but Cherry just burned.

Cherry snapped her finger in my face, bringing me back to the present. Glaring at me, she spit her gum into her hand, before starting to un-wrap another blow pop. This time it was green.

The rusty Keith Urban twin stepped into class, his belt half-way buckled, a lit cigarette hanging from his mouth and holding a lidded-mug in his hand. From his appearance and flimsy gait, I assumed it had to be alcoholic beverage in his mug. Maybe he had yet to adjust to the U.S. way of life and time importance. He was ten minutes late.

After saying Bonjour, he pulled a TV out of the closet and put it in front of the classroom. He held up the series Family Guy and pushed into the DVD player. Most of the boys and some of the girls cheered, until Mr. Versace set the language to French with French subtitles. He slowly moved behind his desk and placed his head on his hands, as if trying to escape the world. Any minute now he'll probably start snoring.

I paid no attention to Family Guy. I tolerated the animated show in English; it was like Paul's favorite show ever. I had absolutely no interest in trying to watch it in

French. Hazel did the class a favor when she jumped out of her chair, stole the remote from off Mr. Versace's desk. He only made a grunting noise. Hazel wiped the remote off, as if it had drool all over it. The class laughed, they all loved her, especially when she changed the dialogue to English and removed the subtitles completely. The students clapped, everyone besides Cherry. I even did. But still had no interest in watching the show, but I did watch Hazel as she took a graceful dancer bow and glided to her seat.

What did Hazel mean be ready at five at my house? How did she know where I lived? Was there some kind of student directory I wasn't privy too? I hadn't remembered filling out some cheerleading application with my address. That was weird.

Or maybe it wasn't weird. Maybe it was some cruel joke to get me back for all my clumsy accidents at her friend's cost. Mercedes hadn't even come back yet from supposedly going to Hazel's locker to get a shirt. Maybe she was getting some cruel prank ready for me, one she text messaged to Hazel when I wasn't looking. As depressed as that made me, it seemed the most likely.

Cherry was in my second period psychology class, but there were other juniors I knew, including the one from tryouts, who was kind enough to let me go before her. Maybe she already made the team, she seemed happy. I never noticed her in my psychology class before; she was actually pretty besides being semi-pale and anorexic-thin.

Cherry and I went to Subway for lunch. This time it was my choice, wanting to avoid the GC crowd, especially Mercedes. She rambled on about how great her library job was and how snowboarding season had just started, even though it was the beginning of October. The Rocky Mountains were already covered in snow.

The rest of the day, I dreaded for five o'clock. Luckily, I didn't see Hazel or Mercedes. And when I saw Sarah in the hall she happily waved at me and pointed to her phone. When I looked behind me, I noticed it was actually me she was waving too. And checking my phone again for the Mile High community web page, I noticed there in my notification window was a friend acceptance from Sarah Ryan. I just about fell over that the second coolest girl in school wanted to be my online friend. But the victory might be short-lived if Mercedes and Hazel ended up at my door tonight, ready to butcher me to pieces and film it for everyone to see. Yes, I'd seen way too many horror movies. Had to blame Cherry for that one!

The clock read four-thirty told me I needed to change out of my pink ribbon pajamas and toss the heavy blankets off my bed. All the worry about tonight was taking a heavy toll on me. Relieved my alarm clock woke me up a half hour ago, only to hit the snooze button a few times.

My legs kept shaking as I changed into my skinny jeans and my favorite yellow top, deciding it best to skip the country boots for now, didn't seem popular here in Colorado. I squeezed my feet into my plaid boots Cherry got for me. Then I went to my vanity mirror and clipped my extensions in, looking better already. Plugging in my straight iron, I waited for it to get warm, while digging in my make-up bag for some rouge lipstick. I needed every second I had.

Time moved fast for the first time all day as I raced to get ready. Plastering the rest of my makeup the way Cherry had showed me, made me feel like one of her Bratz dolls, with too much makeup on. I grabbed a damp rag and rubbed some of it off, especially the purple eye shadow and red cheeks, nobody's cheeks are that red.

Starting with a strand of my real hair, I used the straightening iron and had to re-apply it a couple of times before it started to match the straight dark blonde extension, mixing pretty well with my real hair's bland brown color. The blonde brought out a blue streak in my hazel eyes. Had to admit the new me wasn't half-bad.

I knew they were coming, but it shocked me when I heard a car engine coming up the driveway, five minutes early. My palms started to turn sweaty. I had to check my makeup again before moving the curtains out of the way, at the sight of the two most popular girls in school standing on my front porch, wearing boots and jeans.

My lungs tightened as I watched Sarah tossing her blonde curls at the sight of Paul answering the door. I couldn't see Paul, but who else could it be? He was the only one home. Our parents were at work. Lucky them! I wished I was with them right about now.

A slight knock sounded, before Hazel came straight through the door, not waiting for my reply. I was going to tell her that wasn't cool, but she smiled, melting my sliver of anger. She stood less than five feet away from me and stepped slowly my way. I wanted her to run into my arms like that old classic movie, Dirty Dancing, I may be strong but wasn't sure I could lift her, but in my fantasy it was possible.

My jaw dropped as Sarah and Hazel stood in my messy bedroom, right next to a pile of my dirty, smelly underwear. I pushed them under my bed, but I wasn't sure I was fast and sneaky enough to hide it from them.

I could kill Paul for letting them come up the stairs. My parents were still at work, but I was sure they wouldn't be glued to a video game like Paul and would come get me to come down and not the other way around. Pretty sure any minute now they were going to make fun of my messy, tiny room that could probably fit in some of their immaculately clean closets.

"Your brother let us in, hope you don't mind. And boy is he such a cutie. You're lucky." It was Sarah who apologized, probably reading my sour expression. She landed on the chair in front of my vanity mirror, forming a kissing expression through the mirror. For a second I fantasized the kiss was directed at me. "I wish I had a sexy hunk walking around my house."

"Ewe, didn't think you were into incest?" Hazel scooted over to the window, as if needing to check on her new jaguar.

"I mean for example a hot foreign exchange student or cousin I'm not related too by blood," Sarah corrected herself.

I wondered if they had come to their senses and realized the obvious. They were way out of my league. I worried they were really spying on my brother, one of them having a huge crush on him and they were using me as a way to get to Paul.

"You do like Flowers in the Attic," Hazel smiled.

Sarah threw my stuffed frog that Cherry won for me at a carnival this past summer, hitting Hazel right in the face. She dropped the stuffed frog and went to sit on Sarah, not letting her move while she tickled her.

I was dying to ask the real reason the two most popular girls were in my bedroom, but my usual lack of verbalization skills kept me uninformed.

"You just need one of these and one of these," Sarah said, as she got up from the chair of tickles and opened my closet, pulling out my suede jacket and then grabbed a water bottle I'd left on my dresser, still full of water, yesterday's water, so probably pretty warm. But who cared?

I followed Sarah and Hazel out my bedroom and down my stairs. They both said bye-bye to my brother, who was sitting comfortably on the blue sofa chair in the front room, playing video games. He turned around to see who was speaking to him, his stunned expression classic, even though he had to know they were already there. It seemed the shock had started to wear off slightly as he realized who they were. He'd never seen me hanging out with the in-crowd before. Paul looked as if he wasn't sure he was seeing correctly. Paul rubbed his eyes probably praying when he opened them he'd find out it was in fact real.

Still in shock, I wasn't grasping the situation completely. I fought the urge to rub my eyes, making sure this wasn't a dream.

Hazel grabbed my hand, her touch was smoothing and warm as she said nothing else to Paul and led me out the door. She relaxed my tense muscles and made my legs less like jelly.

Maybe these girls truly had interest in me and not my brother. I sure hoped so. I wasn't sure I could take another rejection, especially since I really liked Hazel. I could stare at her all day and never get bored. She was even more beautiful than the bratz doll Cherry used in place of her. She wore just the right makeup and her hair was perfectly styled with volume with nice waves, as if a hair stylist had done it.

As we reached the semi-coldness of outside, I scanned the driveway, surprised to see a jaguar sitting in my driveway. Not a real one, of course; although that would be just as farfetched. A car almost as expensive as the house we lived in sat on my driveway; shiny and brand new, with a jaguar hood ornament on the large hood and a stuffed jaguar hanging from the rearview mirror. I couldn't believe it. I'd never stepped foot in an expensive car before in my life.

"Don't worry, it won't bite." Hazel casually secured her hand on her hip and then tilted her head to have me follow.

"I take shotgun." Sarah called out as she opened the passenger side of the beige-colored jaguar.

I cautiously climbed in the back. Worried I was being brought to some graveyard to be buried alive. But even though I didn't know Hazel well, what I knew of Sarah was she didn't have a mean bone in her body, so I had to be safe. Didn't I? Then why was there a giant clot in my stomach, as if warning me to not to go with them.

"Are you ready for the experience of your life-time?" Sarah said to me, sounding annoyed, as if she'd repeated herself three times already,

This was definitely it, I wanted to say. Once again not trusting my voice, I nodded.

"You don't talk much, do you? Don't worry, we're going to change all that," she said, as if there was no question they could change me. I wanted to be different. More like them. Less like me.

As Hazel sped the car out of the driveway and got on the main freeway, Hazel and Sarah talked among themselves. I didn't mind, I needed to take a breather, taking it all in. The Jaguar moved faster than any of the other cars, as she swerved in and out of lanes, passing everyone. I was sure we'd be pulled over by a cop in no time.

Passing by a semi-truck so abruptly scared the shit out of me, I clenched the top handle and held on for dear life. The way we were going, the only place I'd have to worry about going to was the after-life.

Sarah turned around, poking her head through the empty space between the two front seats. "Oh my, you're terrified. If Hazel had allowed me to drive, you wouldn't be holding on for dear life and as pale as that boy in that Zombie movie."

"Maybe," Hazel laughed. "Maybe not. You've been in more wrecks than I have and we got our licenses on the same day."

"Oh yea, like one more." Sarah stuck her feet on the dashboard, but Hazel immediately pushed them off.

The fact either of them were in one wreck already scared the hell out of me.

"We there yet?" Luckily, my fright made it easier to not be too concerned with what I say.

"She doth speak." Sarah grinned at me, revealing her slightly crooked teeth, something I'd never noticed about her before.

These girls weren't perfect. Maybe I was with humans after all. I don't know why I was so surprised. What had I expected them to be? The teens from the old series, *Roswell,* they were as beautiful and instead of alien powers they did have unlimited bank accounts.

I breathed in deeply. "Where are we going?"

"It's a secret. If we tell you then we'll have to leave you in the middle of nowhere in an unmarked grave," Hazel said, swerving into the fast lane, just barely dodging the car that was in front of her.

"Teasing," My sigh of relief echoed loudly in the quiet car, causing Sarah and Hazel to laugh. "Rocky mountains, here we come," they both said simultaneously as best friends often do. Maybe they were actually best friends and Mercedes was someone they tolerated. I wasn't sure. I hoped that was true. I liked Sarah a lot more than Mercedes. Who wouldn't?

The winding of the mountains as we got higher and higher in elevation caused my chest to tighten and it became harder to breathe and not just from nerves but from fear of heights and fear of whatever they wanted from me.

When I was about to throw up, they finally exited onto a dirt road. Hazel gratefully slowed down, but the bumpy road was not helping my stomach. I tried to focus on the solid objects both in front of us and from the side window; I heard it helps car sickness. The higher we went up, the more the trees changed; from beautiful autumn colors of greens and reds to no leaves, to snow on the leaves as we reached the top.

Hazel got out of the car and just started yelling and jumping up and down, as if she was cheering in the Mile High Stadium. That would never be my dream. The idea of doing it in high school both excited me and overwhelmed me enough as it was.

Hazel stopped yelling and stood on the edge of the drop-off, making me nervous she would fall. "I want to be cheering for the Denver broncos during their next NFL Championship. I was in diapers when they won their last one." She stretched out her arms, as if she was on top of the *Titanic*. "My Dad cheered while he held me in his arms, saying I was his good luck charm. He had a lot of money on the game. So with me cheering, I'd make those players step up and be winners, nothing but the best baby, nothing but the best."

Hazel turned around, and I tried unsuccessfully to release a sigh of relief. She smiled a wide one, the widest I'd ever seen her smile. "Don't the mountains feel like home?"

Her energy slowly spread to me, causing happiness to swell in my chest. My stomach-ache was dissipating to reasonable level.

Sarah's suddenly twirled around, hands outstretched, singing one of those tunes from *Sound of Music*. It made me laugh.

When I finally came up for air and Sarah had stopped twirling, I asked her, "Where's Mercedes?"

"Who cares?" Hazel asked.

"What about her? She's a bitch and that's putting it mildly," Sarah said, struggling with saying the 'b' word, obviously it wasn't a word she was comfortable using. "Sorry, I just mean she isn't the nicest person in school and she never makes it easy on anyone."

I wanted to ask them why they were even friends with her. From what I've seen she was a good cheerleader, but not one of the best. Maybe it was just because she lived in Aspen Heights, but then again so does Cherry and they weren't close. Maybe they were at one point though, no one exhaled that kind of tension that Hazel and her had, unless they knew each other well.

"We're the ones with all the power, anyway." Hazel stood up on rock and put her hands out *Titanic* style.

Sarah nodded. She released her ponytail, allowing her long, blonde curls to cover her red ears. Her long boots didn't seem super comfortable, but they looked warm. Never seen either of them dress so modestly before. I could no longer see Hazel's tattoo.

"Enough about Mercy, let's do what we came to do because my hands are starting to freeze."

"Well," Sarah started to explain. Then she stopped for a second, as if trying to find the right words. "We brought you up here because we wanted to help you gain more confidence and help train you to become a real cheerleader, not saying you'd be ready by this year, but I'm saying we could help you. And we want to help you. You are the best dancer and gymnast I've ever seen at this school, besides Hazel of course." She quickly corrects herself.

"The first thing we want you to do," Hazel said, taking the reigns. "And the real reason we brought you up here, probably scaring you to extreme, is we are trying to teach you not to be afraid of your voice, to learn like the two of us did, that yelling is fun. Think of the person or people who have made your life a living hell and use your voice to tell them they're pricks."

When I only stood there, waiting for her to continue. Sarah nodded for me to do as she said. I did. But nothing came out but a meek voice, not even a mouse would be scared by that noise.

"No one's going to hear you here," Hazel said, in a nonthreatening way.

But it didn't stop me from feeling threatened. All of a sudden my best dream was turning into my worst nightmare.

"Think of someone you desperately need to send a message to and just let it go, at the top of your lungs, through the diaphragm." Sarah pointed to my chest.

I did what she said, but once again not much came out, only a soft, squeaky noise. My face flushed with embarrassment, relieved I'd gotten rid of some of my blush earlier so I probably didn't look as much like a red apple.

Hazel and Sarah started yelling from each side of me. I wanted their freedom so bad. I wanted to be able to do what seemed to come natural for them. Something still stopped me, debilitating fear or something.

They both held my hands and kept screaming.

Their soothing, friendly touch changed me. Giving me the zap and courage I needed to join in.

Neither of them laughed when my voice came out as a quiet shake. They both only held my hands tighter, as if telling me to keep going and there were no judgments going on up here. Not like a lion or bear is going to care what I sounded like.

Gradually my shaky voice turned louder and louder with every minute, and I was only gaining vitality and energy. Then both of them stopped abruptly, noticing the drastic change in me. Even though they stopped and I knew they stopped to listen to me, it didn't matter because I kept going. I couldn't even recognize my own voice, so confident and free.

I felt alive for the first time in my whole live. I could do anything, be anything. Anything was possible.

My body electrified with excitement, as my voice only got louder. They eventually joined back in.

I screamed with the other two girls, feeling one with them. They essentially were complete strangers but I'd never felt closer to anyone before in my life or closer to me.

For once, I felt in complete control of my voice, it wasn't too soft or coming out in mumbles. I yelled to the Aspen and Cottonwood trees below covered partway in snow. I got so loud an echo ensued. It made me content to her the smoothness in my voice.

"Great job," Sarah said. Hazel had her mouth open in shock.

They both clapped and clapped. I grinned as we they stopped clapping and headed to the Jaguar.

The ride home passed through in a fast and beautiful daze.

When the Jag drove up into my driveway, I couldn't hide my disappointment.

My parents' cars were probably safe inside the garage stalls, a text message chirpy noise sounded.

Something we'd heard all night, but this was the first time Sarah had responded to it. Forming a hard expression, she said. "Mercedes is throwing a fit. She said I'd better be dead."

"She's perfectly capable of watching her sissy alone; she just wants you to take over so she can watch one of her annoying reality shows."

I wasn't sure what the two of them were talking about, something about Mercedes.

"Oh my, I'm way tired of all her BS and demands. She acts like I'm her personal assistant,"

"Well stop putting up with it. I wouldn't."

This argument between the two of them was interesting, but I needed to go to sleep and place a honey-flavored cough drop in my mouth, even though I didn't want the night to end.

I thanked the two girls and politely excused myself. To my shock, Sarah reached in for a hug and then Hazel did the same. Relaxing my posture, I attempted to memorize this moment. Hoping there would be more to come but not counting on it.

The two girls started arguing again while they jumped back in the jag and sped down the driveway. I wanted to stay in Hazel's hug forever.

Chapter Eleven

"I can't believe you spent all night with 'them,'" Cherry said the last word like it tasted sour. She tossed an eggroll in her mouth with blobs of hot sauce dripping from her lips. I was normally the messy one, but she was in a weird mood, almost seeming more stunned than I was about the proceedings of last night. If I hadn't seen it up close and personal, I wouldn't have believed it either.

"Just a few hours, not all night," I said, handing her a napkin. Everything about today seemed strange, people usually handed me a napkin since food always became more of an accessory to me than an edible item.

To make matters even worse, Cherry started into some weird trance. She was reading something off her I-pad. "The jaguar possesses a powerful bite, able to pierce the skull of their prey, allowing them to eat their victim's brain," Her face glazed over, as if in a trance. "They stalk and ambush their prey."

Reaching forward to snap my fingers at Cherry, she jerked backwards. "Where did that come from?" I asked.

She pointed to her lower back and said, "Hazel's tattoo."

Not quite sure when Cherry had lost her mind. She wasn't making any sense. Why did it matter so much how jaguars stalk their prey? It was just a tattoo not a symbol of some deeper meaning, like she can somehow morph into a jaguar and go around stalking and eating the brains of her victims, whether human or animal.

Nothing she's saying explained the real reason why she had such a disliking for Hazel.

A double clap and a few stomps sounded as I followed the noise to see a group of cheerleaders coming into the lunchroom.

Hazel was in the lead, her short black hair in the cutest pigtails and her sexy muscular legs. "Guess who's an Eagle?" She asked, shaking her gold and green pom pom's in my face.

I laughed and then covered my mouth in embarrassment.

"Guess who's an Eagle?" Sarah echoed. She led the JV squad one row behind Varsity as they performed basic cheerleading movement. "We come today to celebrate the addition of our newest cheer sister to the Varsity squad."

"I'm not even a junior." I asked her, trying not to blush or reveal the excitement in my voice.

"Half your classes are, that's good enough in my book especially since your skills are Varsity all the way." Hazel said, dripping a cold look Mercedes way. I wasn't sure where that was coming from.

"You're a total eagle all the way." Eleven cheerleaders chanted around Mercedes, who scowled at me like I had brought her to a sudden death.

"She doesn't deserve what was supposed to be my Varsity spot. She's only been a team member for five seconds."

Ignoring Mercedes, I realized for the first time my cheeks didn't flame or my chest didn't tighten at the attention. I loved it. I loved all of it. Almost all of them seemed to love me and they loved me for my skills. They loved me for me and they wanted me around and to be a part of their team. Not only a team, but the team I'd always wanted to be on. Especially wanting to join the varsity cheer team when I became a senior, but this was even better.

This was the first time I ever really felt accepted by a group of peers. I will always have this moment, no matter what happens. I intended to lock it into my brain for safekeeping.

And things were only getting better as Sarah handed Hazel a wide striped box. She opened it, revealing a cheer uniform and two gold and green pompoms. My heart jumped.

"You're a small, right?" Hazel grinned, revealing her straight white teeth.

Mercedes leaned over, jumping into the conversation. "Oh come on. She's a large all the way."

I hope that extra few pounds I'd gained hadn't made me a large. But then again consider the source. Mercedes would say anything to hurt my feelings. Mercedes picked up the uniform and studied it closer, her scowl deepened like a sink in a swamp. "Hell no, she doesn't deserve that. She's just a sophomore."

"Put a lid on it, Mercy."

The large lunch crowd began clapping again except Mercedes. The lunch cafeteria workers seemed pleased and stopped digging into coleslaw and mashed potatoes buckets to watch what was going on.

"Congratulations Kenzie, you're the newest member of the AH Eagle Varsity team." Hazel whipped her head to the side to signal Mercedes to listen to the rest of her speech. "We need your excellent gymnastics skills if we want to take state this year in the cheerleader competition. No one else can hold a candle to you."

Right then, Mercedes stormed out of the lunchroom, pounding on the cafeteria floor, like a spoiled child, slamming the double doors behind her with a bang. Only a few seconds passed before everyone resumed back to their activity before all the excitement was over.

For me nothing was ever going to go back to normal. I held a varsity uniform in my hand as if I moved it, it would explode into a bomb. This meant I'd be on Hazel's team, spending every afternoon with her, watching her every move and doing my best to mimic it. It was my dream coming true double-time.

I relished in all the attention, enjoying being admired for something other than an A or a near perfect test score. People don't make such a fuss over things like that.

Paul came up to hug me. I cleared a way for him, releasing one of the cheer members I'd never seen before. He reached in, tightly, and hugged me. Finally letting me go so I can catch a breath he whispered to me, "I'm so proud of you, but I've always been proud of you."

I believed my brother. He had always showed me how much he loved me and there was no exception that the twinkle of pride in his eyes was something I'd only seen when I won the all-around in gymnastics a few years back. He'd never cared whether or not I was in the in-crowd or a not; he just wanted me to be happy. And I was the happiest I've ever been in my life. I was pleased to share the best moment of my life with him.

He finally released me, allowing oxygen to flow back to my head. I couldn't believe this. I couldn't believe my luck. This was my dream and I held it in my hand, as if it was a long-lost butterfly. Only I was the butterfly coming out of my cocoon, ready to become somebody in this town and in this school. I was reborn.

Everyone at lunch went back to their normal routine; even the seniors in Varsity joined them, not bothering to go back to class, can't blame them for wanting to skip class.

I was so excited. I could barely sit still. Thinking about how differently my life was going to be now. Will I finally fit in? I know I can do the moves; will I have the pep and the drive? Will I be able to keep up and memorize all the routines?

My long-time dream of being a cheerleader and of being accepted by the popular crowd had finally come true.

Like all dreams that come true, they had to eventually mold and change into reality.

We picked up our trays when the crowd finally died down and threw our trash away, leaving the trays on the belt. We left the cafeteria, getting stopped many times along the way. The embarrassment and shyness seemed to dissipate with each small-talk conversation I had.

Cherry ran ahead, saying she needed to use the restroom before she lost yesterday's food all over the cafeteria floor.

Everything was so wonderful. I could hardly stop smiling, even my jaw hurt from smiling so much. Nothing was ever going to be the same again. No longer will I be an outcast?

I'd spoken way too soon.

Mercedes cornered me as I left through the double doors, pushing me into the walls, her hands on both sides of me. I was tempted to duck and get the bloody hell out of there, as Cherry would say. But too afraid the girl might morph into Jennifer's Body and eat me if I tried to get away, best not to anger the beast. Her nostrils flared, as she whispered deathly, "You. You. Satan's child. You took my spot. You were supposed to take my JV spot so I could get bumped up to Varsity. This time you will pay for sure."

Her words pierced my skin in a hundred small pieces. Still I wasn't afraid of her anymore. I had friends, her friends, on my side.

Cherry came out of the bathroom and saw my face because she opened her mouth to say something in my defense but I stopped her. "You're time will come Mercedes. That is if you're nice to your seniors."

Mercedes looked as if she'd been slapped. I tried to ignore that I almost sounded too bitchy, especially for me. But she needed to hear it. I wasn't going to let people talk to me like that anymore. And Cherry wasn't going to always be around to save me.

Chapter Twelve

All through the night, I woke up for brief periods of time, trembling and sweating from graphic nightmares; one where Mercedes was eating my brains, zombie-style. I could smell the stench and hear her chomping on bites and pieces of the squishy insides of my brain.

In another nightmare, Mercedes turned into a gothic vampire, slowly possessing my body by drinking my blood; until she had total control of my mind and limbs.

Multiple text messages woke me up for the last time around seven, minutes before my alarm. My fingernails were all chewed down to their core. So much for my nice fingernails!

There was one from Sarah and the other from Hazel, basically saying the same thing, 'Everyone's required to wear their cheer uniforms today.' But nothing else, like they'd just forwarded it back and forth; sounded pretty weird to me. With it being a weeknight, there weren't any basketball or football games to cheer at.

I imagined there would be practice but uniforms were costly. My mom never let her students practice in their fancy uniforms unless there was a performance.

An hour later, I walked into class wearing the tight uniform, trying to tug at its seams to get it to stretch out. I couldn't breathe. The green pleated skirt was somewhat short for my taste. I liked things that went to my ankles.

Maybe Mercedes was right. A large was better than a small. But, a medium would do me justice. I needed to slow down on the caramel popcorn, if I can without hurting my Mom's feelings.

Or maybe these uniforms just weren't meant to be baggy and comfortable. The way I normally liked things, besides the new jeans Cherry bought for me, I was used to wearing things purely for comfort. Those days were over though and I needed to deal with my new life.

Determined to enjoy my day, even if Mercedes happened to turn into some kind of supernatural creature and wreck havoc on me. If she tried to mess with me, maybe for once, without Cherry on my side, I will do my own talking. Kill her with kindness and compliments. I didn't know if that worked, but my Mom always said it was the best way to go about things, but I'd always been too quiet to have any kind of response to the teasing and bullying.

Although today was different. Things were way better.

I stumbled my way into French class, wearing a long fuzzy jacket that covered almost everything, including all of the pleated skirt. Something shorter and tighter than anything I'd ever worn before. My breasts showed no matter how many times I tried to lift the gold and white cheerleader vest up. I worried what people might think of my newly shaved and cut-up legs from the sharp razor I borrowed from my Mom's bathroom. I tried to use clear Band-Aids, but all my Mom had in stock had been Care Bear ones. She thought they were so cute, even though I was almost an adult. I needed to remind my mom for the umpteenth time that I had graduated elementary school.

I stepped into a full class, heads turned to look at me. I put my eyes on the ground, where they were most comfortable.

Trying to avoid eye-contact where Mercedes usually sat, I almost missed my dream girl waving at me with one hand as if on a floatation device and patting the seat next to her with the other hand. I'd died and gone to Nirvana; just wish Mercedes wasn't right next to her. What did she have planned for me? Did she have a taser gun in her purse or a can of mace or a bottle of acid for my eyes?

Sitting down, I juggled an untouched bagel in my left hand and a mostly empty cup of coffee in the other, both a total bitch to carry on my bike. I learned how to ride with no hands a long time ago. Not that these popular girls would be the least bit impressed. Since Mercedes and Hazel both drove cars that were possibly in the six-figure range.

Are they going to open their eyes and see that I'm nowhere near the same level as they are just because I can do some fancy gymnastics moves. Of course, Mercedes was already there. She knew I didn't fit in. I couldn't blame her.

Right now, Mercedes stared right through me, as if hoping I'd morph into a ghost and float away. And why was she lucky enough to not have to wear her cheer uniform today? It didn't make sense.

Hazel smiled, revealing a right dimple. "About time, you almost got here after the addict excuse for a teacher."

I wanted to hug the bubbly girl; who caused a happiness to sour through my blood. Everyone in the room noticed me sit down next to Hazel and most of them either glanced at me as if they wanted to touch me or slap me. I loved it. And not a single one of them tried to make fun of me or say anything mean, not even Mercedes, who went back to placing small Simpson character stickers on top of her nails.

I turned around to peek at Cherry; who gave me a toothy grin. But when she seemed to think I'd already twirled back around, she started biting her lips, something she only did when she was nervous or worried.

I wasn't going to let her concern worry me. My life was changing for the better.

"Take this off; you have nothing bad to hide. Mercy's the one with fat thighs." Her response got a good slap from Mercedes. Boy those two enjoyed slapping each other around. And it seemed to hurt. I would never try to hurt Cherry that way even if she hurt my feelings or slapped me. Not that she ever would.

Hazel reached over and tugged the jacket off me while I somewhat helped. But I was scared, scared to reveal so much of me. The Care Bear Band-Aids were the least of my worries. My thighs were too big and I had a belly that wasn't flat, clearly obvious without anything covering half of it.

"Why are we wearing these? I'm so not ready to cheer," I whispered to Hazel.

"Speak up girl, you're a cheerleader now. It's like we're required to be loud and obnoxious." Hazel raised her voice to where the whole class could hear.

Hazel whispered for me to stand up, I took my jacket with me, covering my stomach and my band-aid covered legs.

"Today the Eagle Cheerleaders are wearing their uniforms in honor of our brand-new Varsity cheerleader," Hazel pointed to me before continuing. "She's taking Raven's spot because she ended up moving to Florida. Lucky her, she said she was right on the beach."

Hazel stole the jacket from me and threw it on Mercedes, who grumbled and tossed it out the open window. Great! Might never see that again. I covered my belly button with my hand and tried to fan my face with the other one.

"Show it off, girl," Hazel said, moving my hand away from my belly, "Once again, the gorgeous Mackenzie Harper."

But to my surprise, everyone cheered, waved or complimented me from all over the room, and not just Cherry. Even Mr. Versace came in and waited at the doorway, clapping at me. All the attention flustered me, even though I loved it. I started to fan my face with embarrassment.

Nobody knew I was a lesbian. Nobody knew I was different. Nobody said anything bad about my stringy hair or my zebra height.

I'd even love to be an open lesbian cheerleader, we were probably not too common, and maybe I could even make a statement, sometime in the not too distant future. For now, this was more than good enough.

When I sat back down, my smile was so wide. I'd forgotten to hide my crooked teeth. I slapped my hand across my mouth, fortunately not even Mercedes noticed. She just kept starring at me with a ghoulish look on her face. I kept shuddering, reminding me of my dreams. I wondered if she was really an evil supernatural creature. I did believe in the possiblility of zombie apocalypse.

The French teacher finally arrived and seemed less drunk than usual so he spent the whole class-time in one of his self-imposed monologues. But I was relieved; relieved I didn't have to figure out what to say. I wondered what Mr. Versace's deal was. But I didn't have time to think about him. I had other issues to deal with.

Mercedes and Hazel whispered incessantly during class. I strained uselessly to hear what they were saying, but I couldn't pick up anything. I hoped they weren't fighting about me. Mercedes was already mad at me enough for taking what she thought was her Varsity spot. I definitely didn't want her to have any more reason to hate me.

After the bell rang, even though Mr. Versace was still talking, everyone started leaving.

"Bye-bye, save you a seat at lunch," Hazel said, giving me a half-hug before heading out of the classroom with Mercedes in tow.

True to Hazel's word, I didn't see either of them until lunch time, where Hazel saved me a seat. I told her I had to sit with Cherry, but as I started walking to her, she got up from our usual seat, waved me away and took off through the double door of the lunch room without holding any food in her hand. That was weird, even for her. Maybe she was just dying for a subway sandwich or something. Something we usually did together.

I missed the ease of being with my best friend, but sitting at the cool table was fun, lots of fun. Having my brother only a few seats down from me swelled me with pride and accomplishment. For once, I was as cool as my Paul, if not cooler as he sat talking closely with Travis and another baseball fan. Too bad there weren't any cheerleaders in baseball. That seemed to be what the popular GC crowd consisted of; the combination of cheerleaders and baseball players, probably because they were the only winning sports' team on the boys' side of things. So I heard.

Part of me was uneasy, triggered mostly from Mercedes deliberate avoidance of sitting anywhere near me and pretending I wasn't even there. She almost tried to go through me on the way to reach the ketchup. I wondered when all this Mercedes stuff was going to resolve or if it was all going to come crashing down on my head.

My next two classes were full of sophomore's who looked at me as if I had the answers to the social order. The wannabes followed me around. They asked me useless questions and then complimented me on anything, including my pathetic Care Bears Band-Aids.

Hazel tugged my arm before I could even close my locker door and glided me down the hallway telling me we were headed to a celebration in my honor. I heard Cherry slam our locker door right behind us. Forgetting I had ridden my bike to school, I accepted a ride from Hazel.

"What about practice," I said, savoring the free calm of cold wind. I missed my jacket. I needed to somehow deal with the Mercedes' problem. Too bad murder's illegal and frowned upon. Just Kidding!

Hazel tossed her hand through her pixie black hair. "We don't need practice, especially with you around. We were the best last year and we will be the best this year, just bring your game on tomorrow after practice for some hard work and no uniforms allowed for practice."

I nodded. Noticing the brown Jag in the driveway, under the sign that said Student Body President, I wondered if she just bought that parking spot and position, because I'd never seen her do any work for it, besides the occasional morning announcements. Then again it may be legal to smoke pot here, but the world still revolves around capitalism with a capital M.

Mercedes and Travis were already in the Jag when we got there. Mercedes draped her tan, muscular, Band-Aid free legs out the window. I wasn't sure how she managed that without showing her panties in a skirt that size. For a catholic girl, she was more of a naughty school girl with a cross to keep up appearances.

"Cute nails," I said to Mercedes, who slowly softened her glare. Things were slowly getting better. That's a start. But I had a long ways to go before I thawed her. She scooted her chair up to make room for my legs, but wasn't sure that was a compliment or an insult. I do have long legs.

Travis moved over for me to squeeze next to him in the back seat. I sat next to him but kept a space for a fat cat in the middle of us.

"Hey hot stuff. Where you been hiding?" I thought he had to be mistaken. Boys that hot and athletic never spoke to me. There was no way he was talking to me. But who else could it be, he was staring right at me with a smirk-y smile on his face, expecting me to fall all over him the way other girls did.

"The trash," Mercedes said, but got a bitch slap on her right arm from Hazel for her comment.

So much for the witch melting, I hadn't had a free minute all day to go out and look for my coat, so I was thrilled to see Travis hand it over, "You missing something."

"Yea, we also found it in the trash."

"She's kidding." Hazel called, jumping into the front seat. "I made Mercy go get it or she wouldn't be here with us right now."

Hazel raced down the road as if in a high-speed chase, almost slamming into a few preteen boys on bicycles. I swallowed, deciding to hold onto the handle above the window. After passing my neighborhood as if was a munchkin neighborhood next to their gated mansion community, we entered soon after. She pressed in the code and drove right in, pulling into one of the larger GC houses, almost as big as Cherry's.

By process of elimination, I figured it belonged to Travis or maybe Sarah.

Stepping into a giant front room, with stairs that seemed to go up forever, I was speechless. Well, more than usual. A giant picture of a deer head lined the wall, freaking me out, Cherry would go nuts. She hated hunters for food, so can imagine her distaste of those who hunt for sport.

"Let's go change." Hazel called over her shoulder as she signaled for me to follow her with a bob of her head. I slowly followed her, paying close attention to the pictures of his Dad in his Colorado Rockies uniform with no pictures of a Mom in sight. There was a picture of what looked like an older version of Travis in a Colorado Rockies World Series game.

I followed Hazel and Mercedes to a guest bedroom, three times the size of my regular bedroom, where a few braided baskets of suits rested by the door of all sizes, colors and shapes. Even big convenience stores didn't have such an eclectic collection.

Most of the female suits I found were way too revealing and small. I wasn't about to wear even less than my cheer uniform. I wanted to be comfortable on the outside as well as on the inside.

Hazel easily found a scarlet red color that looked fantastic on her tan skin and full breasts. She even had a butt to show it off, surprisingly so with her skinny frame. I wanted to both touch her and be her at the same time.

We met Travis in the backyard with his covered twelve-sized hot tub. I'd picked out a modest black two-piece that I had to tie tightly in the back to keep my breasts from showing and a bottom that looked more like white and black shorts. Mercedes wore less than any of us, even Travis who had grossly chosen a Speedo; way more than I ever wanted to see from any boy. I sat as far away from him as I could, even if it meant ending up closer to Mercedes. At least Hazel was right next to me, as she pulled out a plastic bag with the word, potpourri written on a yellow masking tape.

"Nothing better than a bowl," she said, holding the smoke and bringing it up to her partway open mouth, where she took a long inhale before releasing. She moaned softly as she enjoys the poison filling up her lungs. I so didn't want any part of this. But what was I to do? If I turned it down, they would think I was a narc or a wimp.

Mercedes took a few inhales before passing it on to me. I took it, without questions. Even though I wasn't up for this, how could I resist. I smoked it, even though my hands shook so bad I almost dropped it.

"Sarah's missing out." Mercedes stuck her topaz-painted toe nails out of the hot tub and leaned back.

That's why Sarah wasn't around and I assumed that was often the case. Sarah and Hazel seemed so close in other ways, but guess not when it came to this sort of thing. I never wanted that to be me. I wanted to prove I wasn't a good girl. I could be dangerous and rebellious while ignoring the guilt tugging at me.

I turned the pipe over to Travis, sitting across from me. "You need to inhale, woman. You got shit." He held out a lighter to light it with one hand and an ashtray with the other, probably so none of the weed will waste away in the water.

I tried it again, inhaling it like I used to need to do with an asthma inhaler, till they found out I was having panic attacks instead. My fingers started burning. Instinctively I threw the pipe down. Luckily it landed in the ashtray Travis was holding out for me and not in the hot tub.

"Don't give it to her again. She's so shaky she's going to drop it all in the fucking hot tub."

"It's my shit I can give all I want to her," Travis said, not the least bit intimidated by her. As a result, he gave me another shot at taking the pipe, but I turned it down.

"She's already ripped anyway, look at her eyes. She can't even take one hit without getting stoned."

"Will you stop it? She's our new friend. And at this point, you're going to be the one to have to leave the crowd. No one in the state has skills as good as hers."

That shut Mercedes up, but not for long."Then I will tell everybody how you threw yourself on top of me in the stands after we won the state finals, even though I don't swing that way."

"Whatever. You have me confused with someone else, whore."

"Slut."

Hazel spit out some mucus, as if the thought was too disgusting to contemplate.

Travis released a long indulgent breath, making circles in the air. "A make-out session between you two sounds smoking hot. What's stopping you now?"

I laughed, but at something else entirely. "Why do you think they call them stands, anyway, if everyone sits? Why don't they just call them sits or then would everybody stand?"

"She's lit," Travis laughed, while placing his arms behind both Mercedes and Hazel simultaneously.

"You're not making any sensibility?" Hazel said, joining in on the hilarious laughing for a dumb joke.

Well, I'd certainly experienced another reason why people might like to call this the mile-high-city, or the mile-high suburb in our case.

Everything felt so easy, probably because of the weed, I loved this night. It was so perfect. The hot water and soothing jets, the feel of Hazel's body close to mine, her hand caressing my leg, going higher and higher than anyone else but my gynecologist had ever gone. "

"I don't know about any of you, but I think it's time to get on the side of the tub before I burn," Mercedes tired to climb up but just fell back in.

"Guess, someone else couldn't handle their weed." It took me awhile to realized I had said that out loud.

"I like this version of you. So laid-back," My cheeks flamed with Hazel's compliment and my legs burned from her touch as she casually moved her hands up to my thighs. My heart kept skipping with the hot tub bubbles.

"Where's the three boy musketeers," Mercedes asked, probably wanting more male attention.

"For now. We made Kenzie's brother one of us."

"Oh yea, he's hot." Mercedes said, causing throw-up to swell in my throat.

"No way. Why would I invite more boys along?"

"You don't need to." Hazel oozed. "You're plenty hot for us."

Mercedes splashed some of the water from her water bottle on him, as if trying to Travis to cool off.

Travis scooted Hazel and Mercedes closer to him. Hazel cuddled up close to him, being the guy she kissed on the lips the first day of school, it made me wonder if they were an actual couple. If so, maybe I was way too late and maybe she wasn't as into girls as much as I thought. But then she moved her hand higher up on my thigh.

"Can you believe this stuff used to be illegal?" Travis said, causing Hazel to move her hand back to herself, as if it mattered if he saw something going on between us.

"I know. All it is s a plant. So essentially plant juice," Mercedes smoked right into Travis's mouth until they were practically kissing. Well, there went my theory that

Travis and Hazel was an official couple. If they were, they were big on the sharing.

I didn't know being cool would turn me into a junkie, legal or not. Here forty minutes or so from the mile-high-city I guess it was better to turn now then to do it in Salt Lake City where people probably got busted for even thinking of doing weed.

Hazel's words echoed how I felt. "It brings you to a different world, feeling like you're floating and rising above all your problems, it's like all your anxiety disappears and everything becomes funny and light." She smoked circles in the air, releasing her hand from my thigh before it got anywhere too close to my privates.

The rest of the night could've lasted forever if I had my choice, especially if Mercedes and Travis were to leave and go do something else, find a room or something far away.

Unfortunately, Hazel never made another move on me in the hot tub or at Travis's house, even though I badly wanted her too.

The night did last a long time. After the hot tub we played in the cold, refreshing sprinklers and then dried off inside, while we ate everything in his counters. When Hazel was sober enough to drive, she offered to take me home. While Travis, with pressure from Hazel, reluctantly offered to walk Mercedes a few houses down.

Something changed when she walked me to my door. It started to feel like an actual date was going on between us. Excitement ran through my veins.

To make things even more date like, Hazel pushed me against the wall, cornering me so I couldn't get out. She laid her lips on mine, as if she hungered for me more than anything. I wiped the drool off my mouth when she finally stopped. I didn't care that my lack of breathing became an issue.

I watched as Hazel merged into the darkness of the night, her feet the only sound on the concrete driveway and then a roar came to life. I couldn't move. Too stunned to collect my thoughts together for movement, my fingers touched my lips, still warm from the kiss of my lifetime. I was never going to wash my lips. I could still smell and feel her blueberry lip gloss on me.

Chapter Thirteen

Ever since the moment I woke up, I'd only thought of Hazel. About the way she smelled of blueberries, the red glimmer in her wide brown eyes and the way I craved kissing the rest of her perfectly symmetrical face.

Getting out of bed slowly, putting one foot in front of the other, I took baby steps. Everything seemed new. The world seemed different. Maybe it was just me.

I retrieved my favorite lavender sweater from my closet, accidently placing it in the garbage. Was I losing it?

I must be way out of it. I collected my sweater from the garbage, without tossing it in the laundry like I should've and placed it over my head. I shook my head, taking it back off before putting a new, red one on. A gift from Cherry so it cost more than the ten dollar shirts I always wear. Then I started to place my boots on the wrong feet. I needed to snap out of it.

Maybe my Columbian Blend coffee would help. I went downstairs to brew some.

Was I depressed or simply obsessed? Obsessed maybe! But why wouldn't I be? I mean damn, that was some kiss.

Much better than any country music video, with me being the one running around barefoot this time, being kissed passionately or driving my girlfriend's big truck. Perhaps if she drove a big truck and I knew how to drive.

I wondered what the kiss meant to Hazel. Was I just one of her benefit buddies? I'd seen her kiss both Mercedes and Travis before, but never with tongue. Last night, she definitely used some tongue, caressing it against mine. Ah the thought was simply amazing! I was surprised I slept at all last night.

Did Hazel like me or did she like Travis? I wasn't sure. I was so confused. The two of them cuddled last night, but I never saw them kiss. It seemed like Hazel and I spent most of the night together. The way Cherry talked about Hazel and Travis this past summer made it clear they had a thing going on. Was it over? I wasn't sure how the whole 'bi' thing worked out. Not my cup of tea.

Hazel could also have a thing going on with Mercedes, even though she denied it. I needed to find out some facts quick. Or maybe I just needed to stop thinking about Hazel for at least five minutes straight so I can focus on something else. Like the coffee I poured as it dripped everywhere, from the counter to the floor.

Damn. Since it was afternoon, my Dad pounded away at some new project in his man cave downstairs and my Mom had left this nice hot pot of coffee for me that now burned my bare feet. I grabbed a towel and started to wipe. Was it possible to still be high?

Must be! It is in my case.

I couldn't neglect my own life while jumping in the Jag with Hazel so to speak. I had advanced classes to study for and a few texts from Cherry.

Searching through the latest texts, disappointment ran through me because none of them were from Hazel.

Cherry told me she was coming over for dinner though. So I needed to let my parents know to add a fruit salad or something similar for dinner. I texted a 'k," with my phone and placed it in my back pocket. The only action I would get today was the vibrations I kept getting from Cherry in the back of my butt pocket.

Staring off into space with the latest issue of *The Denver Tribune*, I tried to read one of my Dad's articles. Thoughts of Hazel drifted back. Was she just high on weed? Would Hazel ever touch me sober? The only way I could find out for sure was to see if she treated me differently when she wasn't high. Then again, what if being high was her middle name?

I tried to remember back to all the other times I saw her, were her eyes bloodshot? I didn't think so. But I couldn't be sure. Plus, there was Visine.

Thinking about weed, the guilt started to attack me. I remember promising my Mom on the day we went to visit her brother in the Utah State Prison, I would never touch illegal drugs or drugs that were illegal for me because of my age.

My Uncle Larry had a long list of drug charges, including selling to minors. I told them I'd never sell to minors. They didn't laugh.

On the way back to Salt Lake City with my Mom driving, I promised my parents I'd never to use drugs or alcohol before I became legal.

Speaking of my Dad, he came up from downstairs carrying a miniature robot he created, "Hey, congrats on making the cheer team."

Reading the surprise on my face, he explained, "Your Mom told me, she was so happy."

I grinned, the guilt relaxing some. At least my parents were proud of me for the time being.

"We need to have a celebratory dinner or something." My dad set his invented robot on the table. "Or you could buy a gift, whatever your heart desires these days?"

Could you buy me a girlfriend, one that started with an H? "That sounds good," I said, with less enthusiasm than I intended.

"What's wrong hon? Looks like you may have a fever." He placed his wrist on my forehead, and kept placing it on and off multiple times, disappointed by what he found out. "You feel hot. I better call Mom."

"I'm fine, really." Yep, Saturday was Mom's busiest day. She probably won't make it in time for dinner tonight with Cherry. I thought now was a good time to bring it up, ask if it was ok if she came over.

"Can Cherry have dinner with us tonight?"

"Sure. That girl's like family. Always welcome."

"Thank you," I said, before sipping some of my coffee.

"Well, let us know when we can come see you at a game." He poured himself a cup of coffee. Only dad and I could drink coffee this late and still sleep at night. Mom had to stop after noon or she was up all night.

"I will. Thanks."

I wanted to ask my dad to wrap me up in his arms so I could tell him about last night and my conflicting emotions. I used to be able to do that with him. But that was before. I wasn't a kid, anymore. Even though I still acted like one on the inside.

My dad studied me closely, as if worried one of my pimples were going to burst into a song or dance any minute now.

He didn't have to say any words for me to know that he was deeply worried about me and for probably good reason. I could've said no to the pot. And I wasn't sure why I didn't. Why was it that important for me to fit in? To be with Hazel? Would she want me if I was a nonsmoker? "I'm fine, Dad, nothing to worry about," I finally said.

My dad sighed deeply, before saying something that had nothing to do with my physical words and everything to do with my internal ones. My dad had the mentally ill in his family, somehow psychic seemed to go hand in hand with the mentally ill. "I may not be the most religious person in the book, because I don't go by any book, besides my AP style guide," he leaned in closer to me, uncrossing his arms, referring to his book; he calls the journalism bible, that's always on his desk. "Most important is no matter who you become, you stay true to what you believe is right, without changing just to fit in."

I nodded, looking away from his loving eyes, trying to ignore him. I wasn't ready to hear it.

"Why don't go you take a shower? It'll make you feel better. I'll order one veggie pizza and one sausage and cheese when Cherry gets here. Paul will be late."

"Okay. After a warm shower. I need to crack my books. Come get me when they arrive."

I was so not in the mood to study right now, but I had no choice. I had a major paper due and two tests coming up. First I needed to call Cherry and not leave out a single detail out about last night. Well, maybe a few.

A few hours later, Cherry, my Dad and I sat around the wooden family table.

"I just think you deserve someone better, that's all." Cherry said, with a mouthful of vegetarian pizza in her mouth, the last piece of that pie. She was never one talented at small talk, especially talk appropriate for family dinners, even if two of my family members were missing.

"Like who?"

Cherry opened her mouth to say something, but then just as quickly closed it. The silence weighed heavily between the three of us, but she'd made it clear she wasn't going to answer me, making me want to strangle her to tell me what she was about to say.

"Who?" I repeated, getting more irritated by the second. Throwing my sausage and cheese pizza angrily back on my plate.

When it was clear Cherry wasn't going to answer any time in this generation, my Dad interrupted, always the peacemaker. "Well, I for one am really happy my daughter here is expanding her social network and finally able to use all the gymnastics and dance she's worked so hard at her whole life." My dad wore an outfit with three different shades of red, his favorite color. His slightly gray hair sat in a mess on top of his head and he grinned, revealing dimples only Paul was lucky enough to inherit.

I loved how it always seemed my Dad could read my mind and how he loved to make things easy for me and make me happy. My parents were angels fallen from heaven, but not because they were too bad, but because they were too good and heaven couldn't keep them. They made me feel safe; that if the world collapsed around me apocalypse-style, my parents would still be there for me, protecting me. Even during a zombie apocalypse. They'd be holding their hands and moaning with me. Didn't know what I would ever do without them. I wished Cherry had what I had, but in the meantime my family had decided to treat her as one of their own.

I wanted to express my feelings to my parents, about how grateful I was they were always on my side and trying to help me. After seeing some of the GC parents, I know Cherry was right. I was lucky, but my shyness even entered into my own home. It always seemed awkward for me to express myself and show my gratitude. I always chose to show it by doing well in school and being home before curfew, not that that was ever a real problem without any friends to hang out with.

My mom was still not back yet, but I felt her presence and concern, I overheard the two of them talking through the vent earlier this morning of their worry for me, about me forming new relationships and not giving into peer pressure.

Now somehow after five minutes of my eating pizza, Cherry had brought up Hazel and how she's displeased with my choice of new partner. Luckily, my Dad never had a problem with my sexuality, unlike Mom had at one point.

"Hazel thinks she can do whatever she wants, when she wants too," Cherry said, not bothering to edit her words on my Dad's account. She also treated him like a Dad.

"I don't think so, never met anyone like her."

"Thank your lucky cards you'll never meet anyone like her again."

Surprised by her meanness and abruptness, especially with my Dad around, I jerked back. She rarely said anything bad about anybody. I wasn't sure how to react, so I kept silent. My dad even seemed stunned by her forcefulness, Cherry always seemed so loving and forgiving of everyone. It didn't seem to fit.

My Dad looked at his phone even though it hadn't beeped or rang. "Got to go pick up your Mom," he said, shoving his fourth piece of pizza in his mouth, without bothering to place his plate in the sink, something he rarely forgot. He must be dying to get out of this awkward moment because he forgot to kiss me on the forehead like he usually did when he left the room.

The two of them shared a car to keep in line with expenses. They hated credit and did their best to live within their means. And their means was nothing like the means of those in the GC neighborhood. "Sucks my parents have to share a car," I complained.

"I wish I had a Dad like yours, or any Dad."

Shame rode through me. Here I was complaining about money when Cherry had lost her own parents. Wait a minute. "Huh?" I asked. I thought both her parents had died; wouldn't one of them include a Dad?

"Just forget about it," she said, picking up her crust-remaining pizza and throwing it away in the garbage disposal, while turning it and the water on.

Why was she so secretive? I'd been like an open book to her, telling her most of my secrets, even about the kiss last night, leaving out any mention of the heavy pot use going on.

Why did she keep so many things hidden and why was I unable to put up a fight? I wanted to be more assertive. That was one of my goals. One I was working on.

My second and even more important goal at this time was trying to figure out what Hazel's kiss meant. I needed to figure out what Hazel wanted and a way to ask her.

But how was I going to do that when I couldn't even be straightforward with my best friend. I can only do so much at once. First, I need to be straight with Cherry.

"Cherry, can I ask you something?" I dropped my uneaten slice of sausage and cheese pizza.

"Do I want to answer?" She asked, cautiously sitting down next to me; picking up a vegetarian slice, playing with the red pepper and the tomato, as if trying to get them to kiss one another.

"Not psychic," I said. "Seriously, what happened to your parents?"

"Some people think certain people don't deserve basic human rights."

I waited for her to say more, the silence weighing heavily between us. The first sign of snow falling on the window pane, I remembered in elementary school how every single snowflake was different. I thought the teacher was just giving us a story to raise our self-esteem. But, the better I get to know people outside my family, the more I realize just how possible that is. People were so different. And even though we've spent almost every day together for four months, there was so much I didn't know about my best friend. Making me wonder if we were even best friends, but I didn't know of anyone besides Sam she confides in.. She hardly ever sees Sam because she's so busy being emancipated and working full-time to support herself.

I wanted her to say more. Find out Cherry's struggles. The sight of her sad blue eyes deeper than ocean water, told me to leave it alone for now. As much as I didn't want to, I listened to the waves.

"Just be careful," Cherry said over her shoulder, before eerily leaving the kitchen.

I wasn't sure how long I sat there; tired from the powerful emotions running through me. What was the deal with Cherry? Clearly what she went through was too painful to talk about, even though it was at least ten years ago.

I couldn't even imagine life without my parents. They were my rock through all of the bullying and teasing from the neighborhood girls who hated me because I wasn't exactly like them.

It finally dawned on me that I hadn't seen Paul all day when he walked into the kitchen wearing an Aspen Heights ball cap and holding a baseball glove. While saying hi, he shoved the last two sausages and cheese slices in his mouth, hardly coming up for air, causing me to dry heave.

Cherry finally came back into the kitchen. "What's taking you so long? Hey Paul," she turned to him, finally noticing his presence.

I watched as the two of them exchanged pleasantries and then got into a heated discussion about the entertainment value on one of the new shows on CW.

"But she's sexy."

"Physical appearance has no value in a show's quality."

"It does when she looks like a hotter Megan Fox."

I ignored them, thinking about Cherry's earlier warning to be careful about Hazel. The memory of her words sent chills down my arms. What did she know that I didn't? Or did she not want me to have friends outside of her. No, Cherry's not like that. Then what was it?

Chapter Fourteen

I watched as Cherry clomped into the lunchroom the next day, clearly on a mission. Her hair pulled into two high braids, holding a thick folder and wearing a shirt with an ice cream sundae on it that read, "Always better with a Cherry on top."

"When did Cherry turn into such a fruitcake?" Hazel said, chomping on a Weight Watchers desert bar.

Being unable to find Cherry earlier for lunch, I sat with the cool table. I wanted to stay close friends with her, no matter what. She meant the world to me and I owed her the world for what she'd done for me.

Ignoring Hazel's devil rays, I waved for her to join us

Glaring at Hazel for her insult Cherry waved at me, but passed by the two of us, and landed next to my brother on the other side of the table. He stood up and the huddled close together at another table, finally taking their seats in an otherwise free table. Since when do they sit at lunch together? Since when do they need to be alone together? Weird.

What the hell's up with them?"

"Oh, my, when did we start using the term fruitcake?" Sarah said, plopping right next to me on my right. She must've been there for some time, but this was the first I noticed her.

"Whats up, fruitcake?" I smiled at her, sighing with relief.

Sarah gave me a funny look.

"Sorry, everyone was saying it. Just peer pressure," I said, trying to avoid her big blue eyes.

Hazel snorted, almost choking on her diet coke she was chugging down. "Have to admit Cherry used to have some kind of decent fashion sense."

Sarah's happy, glowing face fell, "I personally feel that," she placed her hands on her chest, "Cherry's pretty, confident and unafraid to do what makes her happy." Following her gaze over to Paul and Cherry, there seemed to be something else entirely different going on in her mind as she watched the two of them, with a longing that seemed out of place. I tried to remember if Paul had ever mentioned her, but I can't remember. He wasn't in any of my classes since most of his classes were pretty average or like auto mechanic. I can't even drive a car, nonetheless figure out how to put one together.

"Then why don't you date her?" Hazel threw the desert bar, missing the trash can by about a foot. While a new sophomore baseball player immediately picked it up and threw it in the trash, stopping to wait for a thank you, she only waved him away.

"Geez, sometimes I think I'm the only one around her who doesn't swing both ways." Sarah whispered to me, loud enough for Hazel to overhear. I wanted to tell her I would never touch a guy romantically for nothing.

Remembering the way Hazel and Mercedes made fun of Cherry's friend I decided to keep my mouth shut, secretly wishing I could be stronger and less afraid of what others think. More like my best friend, if she was still my best friend? I wished all of us could just be friends, I still had no idea what transpired between Cherry and the cool crowd that only Sarah seemed to still like her.

"Maybe you're in it for the banana, but on Cherry's end not so sure," Hazel said to Sarah, with a hint of jealousy in her voice while she jumped down to go talk to Mercedes and Travis on the other end of the table. None of this lunch was going the way I had hoped. Sitting with the popular table was a dream of mine for so long. I longed for it on my many trips to the bathroom during lunchtime last year. Only to move from one stall to the next so people wouldn't catch on. I guess I never figured I'd desire to go back to hiding in the restroom to avoid all the high emotions that seemed to be going around.

Like, why it wigged me out so much that Cherry and Paul seemed to be ignoring my existence. They'd always gotten along really well, but I never knew them to be hanging out buddies without me. I knew they shared history class together but that was it.

"Huh?" I asked. What was all that about? And why did Hazel seem jealous of Cherry? Why would Cherry not want the banana? She seemed into my brother that was for sure.

Guess Hazel could be jealous. Sure Cherry's house was bigger, but she only lived with relatives, having lost her parents. Plus, it was strange to think Hazel of all people would get jealous of anyone.

Plus, why would she say Cherry was bisexual or gay. There was no way. She was clearly into my brother. Was Hazel into Paul, too? Was I just some pathetic girl that everyone still used to get to my hotter older brother? Had anything changed or was it just all my imagination? If I recall correctly, Hazel seemed pretty bi balanced, into both the genders.

I really needed to get the dish on what's going on over there. Paul and Cherry continued huddling closely. Sometimes I wished Cherry was family, but not sure I wanted her to be with my brother. It bugged me and I wasn't sure why. Maybe I was only irked because Hazel seemed jealous. Jealous of who though? And why?

Everything was so damn confusing.

Like, why hadn't Hazel tried to kiss me again? Or ask me to hang out besides just group lunch? She didn't act like we were a couple, like I hoped she would. She included me in her circle of friends, but was that all we were, just friends?

"Why does she hate Cherry?" I turned to Sarah, who only shrugged, not resolving any of my questions. For once, she didn't seem chatty. Now girl! Now's the time to be chatty! I wanted to scream to her, but shyness was still a problem for me and conflict was an even bigger conflict. I was just getting better at hiding it. Plus, Sarah wasn't a gossiper or someone to speak ill of others.

I started to wish Sarah was with my brother. Anything to get Cherry's paws off him! She was my friend, not his.

I finally understood the expression, "you can't choose who you love."

I started to stare at Hazel. She winked at me, probably noticing me staring at her. Her forever lashes and her knife scar on her left cheek she had yet to explain. There was a lot I didn't know about her; an enigma of sorts. A line of people waited to talk to her, that wasn't unusual. Do I get up in the line and wait for her? Did anyone ever actually land her as a girlfriend? Could I actually become that person for her?

I came home after a lengthy cheerleading practice, mostly watching Mercedes bully the sophomore towel girl from Japan. I'd never met her before, even though she was in my grade. I wasn't sure why we needed a towel girl. I always thought that was some kind of cheerleading myth. But no, and she did just that. She gave us towels and water when we were sweaty and picked up after us.

Maiko wanted to become a cheerleader and study under Hazel. Everyone else but Maiko knew that would probably never happen. She was only a freshman and Hazel would be graduating in less than two years and didn't seem to like Maiko any more than Mercedes did.

When Maiko wasn't around Mercedes and Hazel trash-talked her and it bothered me. It really bothered me, reminding me of painful memories in the past of overhearing similar conversations about me.

I worried about Maiko, trying to get a chance to talk to her and give her some advice. Then again, I wondered who was I to give someone else advice about anything other than how to study and how best to do a front flip. Other than that, I was pretty strapped in the social area and had no clue what I was doing. It was possible they even badmouthed me when I wasn't around, especially at the beginning.

Hazel had led our varsity squad. Sarah led Mercedes and the other JV squad in a different cheer, but Mercedes barely hid her distaste of me in what she believed was her spot on the varsity team.

A confusing situation since the two teams were just right next to each other in the same-semi-small gym room, apparently designed just for us, with mirrors lining the walls as if in a ballet studio.

Didn't make sense that the school seemed to have so much extra money from the rich parents and there were no gymnastics or dance team? What was up with that? Clearly, I wasn't the only talented gymnast or dancer in the room. But I had to be the worst cheerleader, constantly struggling to keep my voice to an audible level.

On the upside, Mercedes or Hazel wasn't paying a lot of attention to my fumbles. I just wasn't into it. I kept thinking about what happened at lunch, and how none of my questions got answered. Hazel seemed deep into the cheer, only commenting to me about increasing my volume ever so often. I was in the back row, and I figured out that was how it would stay for awhile. Mercedes was probably pleased about that one.

Relieved when it was all over and Hazel offered me a ride. This time I'd chosen to have my Mom drop me off at school, just in case there was this chance. I jumped at it.

We rode the rest of the way in silence as her left knee stuck out the open window, even though it was freezing and a rap song played on full blast with loud speakers making me feel the music more than hear it. To make matters even worse, she sped to my house like a shaky person, needing to shoot up.

Hazel pulled up to my modest house, then leaned over real fast and landed a kiss on my lips. Nothing at all fancy, but it was so soft and had me thirsting for more.

"So girl, I've got to swing by and get something. But I'll be back over to your house real soon," she said, as she clicked her Jaguar doors open.

My boots rustling through the fall leaves as I zipped up my jacket, before getting out of the car. Her car was icy cold. I nodded, swallowing down a sarcastic comment about her calling me 'girl.' She had said the word as if she was a part of the mafia or something and I had to keep it a deep, dark secret, even though I had no clue where the hell she was going?

As she sped away, I noticed Cherry's blue Malibu in my driveway. I raced into the house and up the stairs, barely taking a breath. Surprised my open room was completely empty, I sighed loudly. Especially when I heard Cherry's bubbly laugh and no loud metal jams filling up my ears.

Disappointed, I stayed in my room. Not wanting to interrupt the two of them but at the same time wanting to interrupt. Like what the damn was up with them anyway.

Cherry finally noticed me pacing back and forth in the hallway as she came out of Paul's open door. "Hi BFF, you're wondering what I'm doing in here?"

"Kind of yeah," I said, trying to sound casual.

"We're just working on a history assignment together. We have to pair up for an oral report on a time period. We chose the Dark Ages."

I laughed. That sounded like a definite Cherry pick. I was so relieved that they had a good reason to be spending so much time together. Maybe everything could go back to normal that was as normal as it could be with Hazel coming over any minute. That was going to be a bad experience to see the two of them in the same house. I wondered if I should warn Cherry or something. I guess so. She would do the same if I had a problem with someone and they were on their way over.

"Hazel's coming over." I tried to say it like it was the most casual thing ever. But the look of horror spreading across her freckled face told me otherwise.

To my relief, I heard a knock on my door. Saved by the knock! Guess my karma was good.

"I hope that's okay," I said apologetically before I raced down the stairs to see who was behind the front door.

A high-strung Hazel practically jumped into my arms and laid one on me thick. But for some reason this kiss wasn't at all like any of the others. She finally released me and all I could do was cough. "Did you poison me?" I asked, half-joking.

But to my horror, she held a pipe in her hand and a lighter in the other. She lit the pipe and reached for me again. I didn't want to be rude and jump back, even though that was what I felt like doing. This time she got me even better. Now I was going to be good and high for the rest of the night. In front of my parents when they got home and also Cherry and Paul who were more likely to notice. Never underestimate parental denial.

I closed the door behind me with resolve, as she danced in before me. When my parents get home, they were so going to notice the wretched scent.

Hazel pulled me aside in the hallway, throwing me up against the wall and making out with me. Right then and there! Not that I didn't thoroughly enjoy it. It's just the taste of pot made me feel ill and the idea of Cherry and Paul seeing us worried me a great deal. Since Cherry acted like she was a mafia leader or something.

Cherry smirked loud enough to break the two of us apart. Before she headed back into Paul's room, slamming the door behind her. Damn, that was going to take some apologizing later. Then again, how did one say, 'Sorry I was making out with your worst enemy in an open hallway? Well, my hallway. That point could make things a lot easier.

"Who invited Cherry Cheesecake?"

Way more creative than simply fruitcake. I'd give her that. I couldn't even respond with my own witty comment, nothing came to me besides this, "Paul the Pickle."

Hazel narrowed her brown eyes, looking at me like a species different from human. That had sounded way cooler in my head.

We walked into my room. I closed the door behind me, wondering if I should lock it. But my Dad would go ballistic if he figured out it was locked. Better to hope the parents won't notice what was going on when they get home.

"This room is so cute." She said, jumping on my bed with her feet on the pillows. Then she landed on the bed, spreading her legs apart seductively. Wow. I made a mental note as I joined her on the bed, leaving the space of a few bibles in the middle, since I'd rather wait until we were both sober to do anything sexual. Neither of us were anything resembling sober, especially Hazel.

Hazel leaned against the backboard and sat up, biting into her McDonald's apple slices, crunching them into pieces and swallowing them. Apple slices or maybe it was the weed? She slowly finished chomping her apple while picking up one of her phone-type gadgets and typing away. That lasted forever. I picked up my own phone, reading a text from Cherry, my sucky phone just barely sent to me. "I'm coming over 2 study. We should do the caramel popcorn and TV show thingie after."

I responded with, "Sorry about Hazel." And left it at that.

"Who you chatting with?" Hazel scooted closer, leaning over my phone and completely invading my privacy. I closed the screen as fast as possible.

"What's in the cooler?" I changed the subject pointing to the white and gray cooler I'd seen her holding earlier in the day.

"Coors, Travis's Dad now works there. He gets it for me for a decent price. Baseball legend turned Coors employee." She said, drinking it as if she was blood and she was a vampire. Finally coming up for air, she put the cooler in my face, "You want some?"

"No, that's okay" Was she serious? "I'm good here. Thanks to you."

"Sure, anytime."

My family and Cherry caught on so easy to my sarcasm, it surprised me that Hazel couldn't hear the tone in my voice. I wasn't trying to hide it or anything.

"I'm just swillin'?"

Did I want to ask what she was talking about?

Just as I decided it was better for me not to know, she provided the answer for me.

"It means someone is drinking while there chilling. Drinking and chilling."

Hazel seemed to be in love with anything that changed her state of mind. She got up and danced around my room while popping a pill or two in her mouth from the cooler. "Like this?"

That was more like abusing drugs and alcohol. Drinking and abusing. She tried to offer me a pill, but I shook my head. A case of vertigo coming on pissed me off. I'd only wanted a kiss, how could I be so clueless? Her wasted nature being forced upon me, I wasn't pleased. I needed some air. Bad!

I stepped out to the hallway, searching for Cherry. Anything to get out of this drug-infested room would be great right about now.

Cherry stood outside my door in a creepy still fashion, as if she expected me to open the door right then and there.

"You know that's not good for you. I mean there's a reason they call it dope. You can smoke yourself to school resource in a matter of years. So they say?"

"Well, being smart wasn't getting me laid sooo." I said sarcastically, drawing out the o.

Cherry didn't break a smile. "At least open the window and spray some Febreze in there. We can smell it like all the way in Paul's room."

You mean all the way as in right next door, I wanted to say. But she already seemed disappointed in me. I chose not to make it worse. I decided to be vague instead. "I will. This wasn't my choice," I said, walking back into my room, not wanting to see Cherry's reaction.

"Whatever," I heard her call out to me as I closed the door again. This time choosing to do exactly as she said, opening the window and spraying air freshener. I couldn't have my parents mad at me too.

Feeling Hazel's close presence, I turned around, seeing longing and desire in her face. Before I could tell for sure, she leaned in and kissed me hard, in a way that made the world fade away and pleasure only remained. The aggressiveness was a real turn on for me, made me feel like she needed me and wanted me so badly that she couldn't contain herself.

"I want you," she said, jumping on me, leaning so hard I fell back on the bed. It wasn't the three words I wanted to hear, but at this present time it didn't matter. It'd be way too earlier for those words anyway.

She wanted me and that was good enough. Better than good enough, like a fantasy come to life.

In my faded state, I barely noticed she might not remember this in the morning. But I was too high to care. And the room was way too blurry and her hair softer than anything I'd ever felt before. The lights were dancing around as if in a trippy glee musical. The pot was probably laced with something.

Her sweet scent of flavored peach soap mixed in with fabric softener drowned out some of the pot smell.

I couldn't get enough of her. All an intoxicating mix that entranced me. I fell under her spell, there was no turning back. My whole body wanted to scream in ecstasy at her every touch.

I wanted this night to last forever and it almost did.

My mind was elsewhere, some place far away from here, like OZ or Heaven or Nirvana. Whatever! I didn't care. I was happier than I'd been in months, but I wasn't sure if it was real happiness or just escaping into another place. I felt like a completely different person.

My Mom's voice brought me back to the harshness of reality. Lucky Hazel had hidden her now empty pipe in my top drawer and had closed her cooler Luckily, I'd taken Cherry's advice as well.

"You okay, honey?"

"We're fine." I said, trying to act normal, as I sat up on my bed. Hazel didn't bother to hide her revealing tank top. My Mom picked up her Prada long-sleeved top from off the floor.

"This is a nice top. How much was it?"

OMG. Just be a normal Mom and get mad or something. If it was Cherry, she would've been shouting from the walls but this was the most popular girl in school and she knew it and head of the cheerleading squad. It was her job to know who made the nearby schools' teams and who didn't.

My Mom was ecstatic when she heard I made cheerleading, I guess some of the happiness from it still rubbed off on her and being perfectly ok with having a gay daughter. I mean more than okay. She told her friends all the time in Utah that she had a gay daughter and if they weren't okay with it, they could make a new friend. Some of them chose that option. I wasn't sure if it was because of the scary openness or because of their religious beliefs. "You need to keep this door open a crack, as I tell Paul every time I can."

"We will. Thanks new Mom."

I cringed, but Mom only smiled wide, "So nice to see you around here. Hazel it is?"

"That me." She said in her bubbly voice. Didn't know she had such a bubbly voice.

Hazel lived and breathed confidence, nothing seemed to faze her. She acted as if the swords and knives will break in her path and fall at her feet. Was she afraid of anything?.

She laughed with relief after my Mom walked away, leaving the door open. I couldn't share her response. I was surprised she hadn't at least pulled me aside for one of her peer pressure discussions."

Either way, I would never go back to my cocoon. Never! I was out in the real world, actually holding down real conversations and experiencing life for the first time. So what if I broke a few rules to do it?

I watched as Hazel picked up a peach marker, unscrewed the lid and started to apply the marker to her lips. "Is that better?" She took way more puffs than me, and it was starting to show, plus the pills, plus the alcohol. How was she even laying down straight?

"Um, that's not lipstick much." I twirled around, unable to sit still on this stuff. I often have strange reactions to drugs. My chemical make-up was way messed up. One reason I barely even used over-the-counter drugs. And another reason was I never had the opportunity to use recreational drugs before. Drugs were what people did who were invited to parties and hang-out sessions. Maybe with me referring to them as hangout sessions didn't help any.

"As long as it looks pretty, I don't much care." She drew more peach marker on her lips and then started plastering the top of her eyelids.

I wanted to tell her it looked pretty, but it looked kind of silly, not in a good way. Instead I began laughing uncontrollably until I had no clue what I was laughing about. Hazel looked offended for five minutes before laughing with me.

The mood changed drastically as Hazel turned solemn. I followed her eyes out the window as the full moon came out from under a massive rain cloud. I could almost smell the pre-rain. The rain smell was always so comforting. Reminding me of days my Dad would read the family a story. We were quite the old-fashioned family at times.

"I'm so jealous of you," Hazel collapsed on my bed like a corpse with bloodshot eyes.

She must've read my stunned expression as she explained further. "I watched that first day you moved in. I was in my Jag, going for a drive, anything to get away from my Mom. And the way your parents and brother packed everything inside, like an actual real family." Hazel pulled my comforter over her loose skirt and tank-top. "I'm just my Mom's drug supplier and she only keeps me around for when I turn eighteen. When the house and almost all the money goes to me, she's hoping I will pay her bills for her and keep her in the house. My dad never trusted her, not that he ever trusted me either, thought we were both sluts, when he was the real slut, sleeping with anything in Mountain Shadows with a pulse."

Hazel closed her eyelids and went still as a line at Walmart. She began snoring almost immediately, peach marker outlining her once pretty face.

I imagined Hazel's demands were extensive, between being captain of the Eagles and president of the entire school. Her only recluse must be drugs to escape reality.

Never did I think my dream girl with my dream life could be more miserable than me or have such a rotten home life. Now I knew anything was possible.

Never in a thousand years, did I ever think Hazel would ever be jealous of a girl like me. I could easily understand her being jealous of Cherry, being so confident and self-assured. What was so great about me?

I had something girls like her envied. It shocked me even though it made sense in a way. I used to think I could give up my family if I could just be popular, but when it came down to it, I would choose my family. I loved them more than anything and they loved me. Hazel didn't know what that was like. It was really sad.

I didn't want my parents to be disappointed that Hazel ended up sleeping in my bed. So I blew up the mattress pad and slept on the floor as I do when Cherry is too tired to drive home.

Hazel snoring started up again, for such a small girl; her snore had to be heard throughout all of the bedrooms.

Maybe there was some way my family could adopt both Hazel and Cherry, but those two would fight until the death. There wasn't any happily ever after going to happen with my best friend hating my sort of girlfriend and vice versa.

Almost as soon as I collapsed down on my air mattress, sobriety began taking over and I realized what a huge mistake I'd made.

What had I gotten myself into? Part of me wasn't even sure how compatible Hazel and I were? Sure she gave me the shivers every time she tried to touch me, but sometimes she drugged me too, while being sneaky about it. No matter how much I tried to rationalize that behavior, I couldn't. It wasn't right of her to do that and it wasn't right of her to pop my cherry, so to speak, afterwards. We were both stoned, but she never asked if I even wanted weed. Then again I could've pushed her away when I had the chance. Cherry would have the guts. She didn't care if Hazel or anyone liked her or not.

Speaking of Cherry, there was no doubt in my mind she always had my best interest at heart and would never bring me down to her level. She was too high to be brought down, even by my former goody girl nature.

Hazel, on the other hand, what was she after? I knew who had my best interest. I wasn't a fool. I just wasn't sure.

I still wanted a romance with Hazel; she's the only one who ever gave me fireworks. But at what cost? Do I have to turn into someone I don't want to be in order to be the person who gets to be with her?

Chapter Fifteen

A screaming Hazel woke me, startling me almost to death. What the hell was with her? Did someone die or have a heart attack? God, I hope my family was okay.

I watched as Hazel tore off the covers and jumped up, her pixie hair standing on its ends, like a clown wig. Without make-up, she looked two years younger. Veins seemed to be popping out of her arms. Well, at least she didn't shoot up. Now that was really dangerous and addicting.

"I'm going to be late for French class," Hazel's panicky voice probably reached into my parents' room. Luckily, my parents were likely working or my Mom was in her daily morning Pilates class.

I wanted to correct her, add a 'we' in there somewhere. She forgot somehow I shared the same class with her. Or did she just not care. I'd never seen this side of Hazel. Didn't even know she had a crazy side. I was starting to think maybe everyone was a somewhat crazy.

"Don't you have an alarm?" she asked, searching around the room until she found my Minnie Mouse alarm clock. She followed the cord until it ended right before the plugin. Hazel probably ripped the cord out this morning as the alarm was going off. I slept through the whole thing so I didn't know for sure what had happened. Although I never unplug my alarm in my sleep, then again I probably still had pot in my system, but I hadn't unplugged it. Plus the plug-in was way closer to her.

Hazel had a theory; more than a theory, closer to a fact in her mind. "I can't believe you did this to me. That's my favorite class, the only class I love. I want to be a French major at UCLA and eventually a French translator or model, maybe both. I could be a model, right?"

"Oui,"

"Thanks." She once again didn't catch the sarcasm in my voice. She was certainly pretty enough, but she was at least five inches shorter than me.

I stood up from my mattress pad, my mouth hanging open. What do I say to that? She acted as if I had destroyed her Jag, not caused her to miss twenty minutes of French class. When it was probably her fault to begin with, not that she seemed to be taking any of the blame. I mean it was just twenty minutes.

And I never unplug my alarm for anything, unless my Mom had come into clean. Sometimes she did. But one look around the messy room, with clothes piled everywhere told me that wasn't what had happened. Not knowing what to say, I said, "Sorry." I knew I wasn't guilty, but convincing a hysterical Hazel seemed downright dumb.

Hazel rolls her eyes and said, "Well sorry isn't going to get me there twenty minutes ago."

Nasty! "Well being snippy isn't going to get you there twenty minutes ago either," I mumbled under my breath.

I was about to lose my cool and snap at her. Knowing she could make my life a living apocalypse, I decided not to do it. Instead I decided to apologize again, even though I wasn't sorry. She should be apologizing to me. "Sorry." It came out meek. Still in my outfit from yesterday, and my tangled extensions caused my scalp to itch. I wanted to scream. Normally I take the extensions out before bedtime but I was too embarrassed to do that with Hazel around.

Collecting the rest of her belongings, Hazel raced out of my room. I followed her and so did my dog, Willow. She came running out of my Mom's room to bark at Hazel's quick and sudden movements, clearly not pleased.

Willow wasn't a fan of Hazel. She looked ready to bite as she started nipping at her feet while growling and barking. I tried to get her to stop by telling her to 'stay' but she wouldn't sit still enough for me to pick her up and place her back in my Mom's room.

"If you don't get that dog away from me and fast, I'm going to kick it."

And I'll kick you, I wanted to add. I jumped down to pick her up. How could anyone hit a dog? What was her problem? I'd never seen Hazel like this before. She was acting more than crazy. Criminal. It was a felony to kick a poor, defenseless dog.

I followed Hazel out the front door, hoping she would somehow realize I too needed a ride to that place we both go and to that class we both go too. Her jag gleamed in the morning light, only pissing me off further. Now only was everything she did apparently my fault, but she even drove an actual vehicle with four wheels that cost more than my house, while I just had a rundown bicycle.

Hazel got in her car, clicking the visor down and staring into the vanity mirror. "Holly hell, I look like I slept in a ditch." She frantically searched for something in her car, coming up with a brush and a glittery purple makeup bag. Putting the visor down, she brushed her hair and added volume and length to her already long eyelashes.

Without bothering to offer me a ride, Hazel finished her beauty-on-the-go regime and backed out of the driveway with a scowl on her face, as if I'd ruined her life.

Was she ever going to forgive me? I couldn't understand how this morning was my entire fault, but I still wanted her to forgive me.

What I wanted now was coffee. Bad!

If I take my bike there was no way I'd make it to any of French class. So I didn't bother. I went into the kitchen and poured myself a cup of Columbian coffee and began picking at one of the glazed donuts on the counter. Maybe if I eat, what just happened will make more sense?

Doubt it. Highly doubt it.

How could she just leave me like that, on top of blaming me for everything? What was her deal? Maybe she was crazy. Why couldn't she take some responsibility for her own actions? She was the one faded beyond belief and who shouldn't have even slept over in the first place.

I didn't even want to know what my Dad thought about it. I was sure he'd make her come over for dinner or something after telling me that guests need to be announced.

When I got back to my room, after placing Willow on my bed, I got a text. Hoping it was Hazel apologizing, I ran for my phone, right next to my unplugged alarm clock.

But it was only from Cherry and it read, "Why are you so late? There's a pop quiz today." Great, French and driver's education were my two hardest classes. I didn't want to get my first B ever. At least report cards weren't issued for a couple more months; I could see my extra credit list piling up.

I can't afford a decent education without a full-ride scholarship or close to it? I wish I had the luxury of rich parents to get me into a top notch school and not have to worry about getting all A's on every single report card. It was exhausting and I haven't exactly been studying a sufficient amount lately.

I texted Cherry back, saying I'll be right over for Psychology class, the one we shared together with no other juniors or sophomores we both knew, besides Sarah. I would have to come up with some lame excuse of receiving my monthly scarlet letter for my French teacher. That kind of thing made men just as squeamish as boys. My brother won't even stand in line with my Mom and I when we're buying tampons and mini-pads. Maybe Mr.

Versace will allow me to retake the quiz just to get me to shut up. Here's to hoping.

Or maybe I should just promise him I'll buy him a keg of beer when I turn of age. As my dad always said, 'you have to think about your audience.' I figured out that wasn't just true in writing news articles.

I needed to stay the hell away from Hazel for the rest of the day. So that included a suggestion to go to Subway for Cherry. I pulled out my phone from my back pocket and texted her.

In response, she sent me a smiley face. Not that I was in the mood to eat. My donut barely got touched, but my coffee was all gone. I poured another glass and started to gulp, fully intending to drink the rest of the pot of coffee before I left for psychology class. Right now sluggish was my middle name.

At least psychology was my ultimate favorite class. The way the mind works had always fascinated me. I wanted to understand the way other people think and know why it is people behave the way they do. What causes them to make that horrible life-ending decision to kill their best friend or their girlfriends? After this morning, I had some inkling of why someone would kill their semi-girlfriends. Kidding!

I started getting ready for class; I'd have to leave in a few minutes just to make it to psychology.

To make matters worse, as I started riding my bike to school, I noticed someone was following me. I turned around to see a shiny red Mercedes. If things were supposed to be better than last year, I wasn't sure. It was starting to look an awful lot like my freshman year.

She drove her car super close to me, swerving to almost run me over. Landing inches away from my bike, I jumped into the bushes as my bike went on without me, collapsing on top of me in a matter of seconds.

Mercedes reached out the passenger door throwing a big gulp at me, glee-style. Covering my brand new jeans from Cherry in what looked like red mountain dew. I'll get her back though. Somehow. Someway. She was going down for this.

This was starting to turn into a Utah rerun of 'Mackenzie the loser.' But I refused to cry. I decided to instead take a long breath and realize things were not as bad as before. I was still a cheerleader, maybe not for long. I had Cherry. Hazel probably will forgive me. So what if Mercedes never did? Not everyone had to like me.

I wiped off what soda I could with my hands and used a wet wipe from my backpack to do the rest. I was wet and it looked like I had peed. By the time I get to school, it should be dry. Hopefully!

If it weren't for psychology class, I'd just go back home and dwell in psychotic thoughts of how to get even with Mercedes. At least I'd see Cherry soon. She always put things in perspective and made them seem not so horrible.

Later, at lunch we were sitting in our favorite booth in the back at Subway. A booth always deserted because it was right by a cold spot, but we loved it. This way nobody could spy on us.

Cherry kept pointing at her cheek. It took me forever to realize I had a gob of mayonnaise on my right cheek. I wiped it up with my napkin, feeling dumb. Psychology class was awesome, Sarah sat by Cherry and I and we all talked for a bit before and after class. At least Sarah seemed perfectly nice and even-tempered. Maybe everyone wasn't crazy after all. Cherry never struck a crazy cord in me either. Well besides the way she had to go to every single McDonalds to collect all the toys she loved, like the Wizard of Oz and Smurfs collections. Did she realize she was sixteen?

But when I saw Hazel in the hall I ducked behind Cherry so she wouldn't see me and she didn't. As usual

Hazel glided down the hallway with the world seemingly at her heels wanting her attention. I wanted to know what her fans would think if they were here this morning and they were being blamed for something they didn't do.

Even though her temper wasn't fun and was unaccounted for I still wanted her to be mine. Hazel was so passionate and made all kinds of fire run through my veins. No one else had ever done that for me.

For now I avoided her, better to keep my distance. Relieved to be sitting at a booth in Subway I vented to my best friend. Plus I had a few questions for Cherry. Like if she had a thing going on with my brother.

"So what you doing with my brother?" I asked, unafraid to say what's on my mind with Cherry.

A cucumber dropped onto Cherry's mouth from her veggie delight sandwich. "Ewe, what do you think I'm doing?"

"Do you have a crush on him?" I figured the direct approach might work better with her since nothing else had seemed to work in the past to get her to dish.

"He's like blood," she finally said, shrugging.

"Like blood with benefits?"

"Gross. You are starting to sound like one of those cheerleaders." Cherry placed her sandwich down as if eating anymore was going to poison her. "Not everyone's going to find true love in high school. Some of us know there's life beyond."

"I know that."

Pushing her vegetarian meal away, Cherry said. "You also know that cheerleaders are the least likely group of athletes to continue on to college."

"Bullshit," I said, knowing for a fact or from all the cheerleading magazines I read that most girls not only go on to college, but some end up cheering for Ivy leagues. I wasn't going to waste my breath. "You're acting like they all drop out because they get pregnant or something."

"I didn't say that. Let's just drop it."

"It's not like I'm going to be the first one to go to an Ivy league school. Cheerleaders are everywhere."

"O-kay." Cherry drew out the first letter, getting up from the table and then tossing her meal into the trash, obviously disagreeing but refusing to argue anymore. I was ready to keep fighting with her, but I always got too steamed in arguments.

"You can't judge a group of people like that. That's not even like you." I said, my refusal to drop it getting the better of me. I could feel my temperature rising.

Cherry came back to the booth and sat next to me. She twirled a strand of my hair. "Wow, you've got some strong hostility hidden under your shy décor."

I laughed, even though I caught on, realizing she meant for me to drop the subject and stop asking so many questions. It was just that I hadn't been around for the past fourteen plus years and had no idea what went on before I got here to Mountain Shadows.

I figured I could ask Sarah. They were neighbors their whole life? They had to have birthday parties and other events the two of them attended together? Even just stepping outside their door, or riding their bike, they had to have run into each other. Can they be neighbors for fourteen some years and not know anything about one another.

She unwrapped a green blow pop and placed it in her mouth, probably to signal the end of the conversation. It's kind of funny when she's done talking; she always tended to shove something in her mouth.

As per usual, I was left wanting more answers. She popped her blow pop out and grinned, her Cheshire cat smile, about to say something.

I counted the seconds, waiting for her to say something. Anything will help. Anything to understand what was with all this secrecy and why was she afraid to explain it to her own best friend. What happened in her past to make her so afraid?

Maybe I need to major in psychology in whatever college I end up with in a few years. I needed something to help me understand Cherry or Hazel's unusual behavior. Hazel's behavior even bordered on sociopathic maybe; according to Ms. Romero those types of people blame everyone else for their problems.

Or it could possibly be the drug use? THC is a mild form of acid that slowly destroys your mind, causing hallucinations and paranoia. Maybe she had thought I was trying to hurt her by pulling out the alarm. Who knows?

I will figure it out soon. Hopefully it was just the drugs and not Hazel's personality. I don't expect her to be perfect but I do expect her to be fair.

Chapter Sixteen

I raced my way to cheerleading practice; we were going to make sure everything was right before the game in a few hours. I hadn't had time all day to talk with Sarah alone. Maybe if I get there really early I'll get my chance. I especially didn't want Hazel around, or anybody that might think it was weird I had so many questions about Cherry and her past.

When I stepped into the gym, it was already packed.

"Where you been all day?" Hazel asked with a straight face.

She couldn't possibly be serious. She didn't drive me to school or text me, or make any real effort to see me all day long. What the freak was she talking about?

Still all seemed to be forgiven in Hazel's world. She kissed me briefly on the mouth before started to lead the cheer.

But I was lost, I couldn't keep up. Psychologically I was off and that made it hard to keep up with the cheerleading moves.   I was like a kid on the deep end of the pool, trying to keep my head above water. When everything went Hazel's way, she was amazing to be around, but she had a darker side to her, one that gave me the chills and was affecting my cheer moves.

But to my surprise, Hazel said nothing. Maybe everything got resolved. Somehow without me, she'd gotten over her bitchy morning side. Maybe that was just a morning thing.

I soon found out otherwise.

Ms. Romero taught us in class that everyone had a dark side. Maybe. Maybe not. I ripped off a Chap-stick from Walgreens before. Sure, I forgot to pay for it, but I never went back to the store later when I realized it.

Also, nobody was perfect, that was common knowledge, not necessary to point out in school textbooks.

My first real game was in two hours and I wasn't ready. My nerves were fried and my bones weren't cooperating. Luckily, Hazel seemed back in a good mood, at least toward me. Her bad mood was directed at the towel girl again. Poor Maiko!

"Human repellant, you need desperately to know how to fold a towel. You are the towel girl, isn't that your job. Once over and then doubled." Hazel said, knocking over the cart, dropping towels all over the place. "Fold them right."

I noticed a hint of pleasure in her voice, she enjoyed causing pain. Isn't that what Ms. Romero calls a sociopath? Those who enjoy hurting others without any real guilt or remorse, I wasn't sure I could fall in love with someone who enjoyed causing pain. That wasn't me. I never take pleasure in other people's misery, even if they've hurt me. I don't want anybody to feel pain. But I'm a goodie-goodie. Hazel was something else entirely. I just wasn't sure what that was, but I was determined to find out. I wanted her to still be the girl of my dreams.

The other cheerleaders seemed afraid of Hazel, even more than they were scared of Mercedes. Sarah and Hazel were right that day in the mountains; they were the ones with the real power when it came down to it. But Sarah ruled with kindness and an even temperament, while Hazel seemed ready to lose it on anyone who crossed her. And I wasn't above to being on that blood list as the morning proved.

I had to admit on occasion she did make me pretty nervous. I still wanted to be with her. I think I love her and someday soon she'll admit she loves me too. I hope so. We will hope on a mower, like my favorite movie, "Can't Buy Me Love." I'll be Amanda Peterson and she'll turn

into a much prettier and feminine version of Patrick
Dempsey. Happily ever after

But this wasn't fiction or a good eighties movie, this
was real life. Nobody would create a story about my life.
Why couldn't my life be more like the movies? Real life's
about not setting alarms and being ignored all day.

"We're going to get some salad before the game,"
Hazel said, inviting the cheer team, while glaring at Maiko,
making it clear she wasn't invited. "So you can clean up
this mess." She said, while pushing over a tub of Mr.
Clean and burning hot water. I know because some of it
reached to my feet.

As delicious as green lettuce sounded, I had to pass.
"I'm going to stay behind and work on the routine." I
landed the routine a few practices ago. My years working
with my Mom on dance and gymnastics floor routines had
way paid off. But Maiko needed my help. Because of
Hazel's temper, there were still towels, wet and dry, all
over the floor on top of the extreme water mess and
granola bars and diet drinks everywhere.

"Okay, good for you," Hazel said. Wasn't sure what
she meant by that one. Maybe she's finally admitting I
suck, or at least I did today. There was just a lot on my
mind.

"I'm going to stay too." Sarah said, to my surprise. Probably felt bad for Maiko, too.

The other cheerleaders glided out of the gym.

Relieved Sarah was staying back because I needed to talk to her about both Hazel and Cherry's behavior. Maybe I can finally get some answers from a neighbor who grew up with both of them and could have some real insight into what's going on in their minds.

I approached Sarah cautiously, while carrying a pile of towels to fold. "Hi cutie," she said to me.

"You both really don't have to help me. This is my job," Maiko interrupted.

"We insist," Sarah said, helping Maiko carry a thick cooler full of Gatorade. Since it wasn't sugar free, nobody had touched it. They carried it outside the side door, dumping it all over the grass. Nice red grass.

"I can get the rest," she said to both of us.

"It's no problem-o." I said, getting a mop from the janitor closet.

Maiko kept shaking her head, but allowed us to help. There was still water and towels everywhere.

Finally the huge mess was cleaned up and we had twenty minutes before we had to be outside by the bleachers for the football game. I sure hoped I was prepared. My nerves were all kinds of shot and I could barely breathe?

"You okay?" Sarah came to sit next to me in the locker room. We came there to get our pom poms from our gym lockers.

The dizziness caused me to fall slightly over. Sarah caught me. "Do you need to sit this one out, I can talk Hazel into letting me."

"No," I said, too abruptly.

"She's not as scary as she seems."

"What's the deal?" I blurted out, knowing I wasn't making much sense.

Sarah sat down and sighed heavily, before responding. "You mean with Hazel?" I nodded, so she continued. "She used to be so nice. Hazel, Cherry and I were the best of friends. Then Mercedes moved into town and something happened to Hazel, something changed inside of her. Right about the time her father moved out, leaving her all alone to deal with her Mom's drug habit. It's really sad, actually. Cherry stopped being her friend because she did something really mean to her."

"What was that?" I asked, dying to know.

"Well it was more Mercedes, but Hazel didn't help any. I can't tell you because then I'd be revealing a secret of Cherry's I'd promised to keep it a secret. Only our circle of friends knew and Mercedes was sworn to secrecy with blood. And she's superstitious so that was the only thing that worked to keep her quiet."

"That's okay." I said, even though I wanted more than anything to know what happened. I had to cut my losses. I'd actually found out more information than I expected from Sarah. Maybe she'd finally realized I deserved to know at least some of what was going on around me.

I followed Sarah to the gym, while holding my gold and green pompoms'. I never thought this day would come. Me as a cheerleader! I could hardly contain my excitement and my nerves all at once.

Well, found out some disturbing news about Hazel and Cherry. I can't for the life of me imagine the two of them being best friends and for years. It didn't make sense. Cherry always danced to the tune of her own rhythm. I couldn't imagine her following the crowd. But maybe that was what happened. She did something to piss Hazel or Mercedes off, something that bothered them enough to end their friendship.

Cheering at the game was everything I thought it would be. To be right behind Hazel, as I watched her short pigtails bobbing up and down was the biggest rush. While the large crowd of parents, students and just neighborhood fans yelled and screamed along with us.

I moved effortlessly and easily, without much thought, capable of doing things the other cheerleaders couldn't. During a short freestyle moment I performed fancy flips and twists, the crowd cheered.

Power was something I never really craved, but it was fun. We led the whole stadium in a few cheers that were causing me to feel exhilaratingly powerful. I barely noticed Mercedes pouting and occasionally flipping me off when I looked directly at her. She hid it the best she could by brushing her hair with her middle finger so none of the other cheerleaders or football fans would notice.

I would feel bad for taking her place, if she wasn't such a biatch.

This made me feel necessary. Something I rarely felt around Hazel. She didn't need me. Sometimes she wanted me real bad though on a physical level. But how could a girl like her need me. No one seemed above or beyond her possibilities. She exuded power with a comfortable charm. Just as easy as Hazel could build someone up, she could just as easy tear them down.

Sarah and the other JV cheerleaders took over the basketball games for us. So they sat in the sidelines cheering us on and the crowd from the stands. Sarah kept lifting up the sides of her lips to tell me to smile more. I did every time I saw her. But then it became too easy. And all I could do was smile.

Maiko ran ragged getting us drinks and towels between breaks, with only a few thank you responses coming her way. But we were all busy, I fumbled a few times, it was hard to keep memorized every moment of every routine, even if I did grow up training how to do it.

Why did Maiko work so hard? Did she actually think this was the way to get on the squad next year for her sophomore year? Most of the cheerleaders treated her as if she were beneath them, especially Hazel.

I was disappointed when the game was over. Sarah congratulated me on a job well done. Hazel said nothing, which may be in her world a good thing. So many people came up to me and the rest of the squad to tell us what a good job we did.

I got almost as much attention as Hazel, who seemed bugged by the fact people interrupted her to go talk to me. She'd slam her right foot and say something like, "I was talking here."

Hazel finally gave up and came over to me, starting to claim she was the one who found me and that I'd just come from a school in Utah of all places, as if all my talent was somehow because of her doing.

Although I did owe Hazel a lot if it weren't for her and Sarah and their ability to work with my vocal weakness, I'd never been on the squad and I wouldn't be able to share my talent with other people. Hazel literally transformed me from somewhat invisible sidekick of Cherry to a popular girl almost everyone noticed. I owed her and Sarah a big thank you.

After the game, I stayed, doing as Hazel wished. Not worth a fight. But I was ticked off. I didn't understand. I thought Hazel wanted me. But then why did she obviously need the class clown telling her how wonderful she was. Who cared what he thought? I sure didn't.Any minute the class clown was going to start salivating. It really looked like she needed to turn him down. Like maybe right now

He started to stick his tongue out, like ready to lick her ear and that was my call. "Hazel, we really need to get going, we're late." I pointed to my cowgirl watch.

She lifted her forefinger, signaling me to wait a few moments. I sighed, without bothering to hide it; sitting down on the steps, expecting to wait awhile. Guess things were just not as green as I thought they would be on the other side of the fence.

Hazel drew in attention like a bee to a hive. Unlike me, she seemed to relish in it, like it was the best drug ever. I hated it. I wanted all the horny dudes to go away. Hazel politely encouraged and continued them on, even flirted with the cuter ones, ignoring my presence. I thought I even heard her give her real number out a few times to the hotter ones.

What the hell did that mean for us? She'd hook up with any boy that was cute. I wasn't sure I liked the whole bisexual thing; I wanted a girlfriend that only wanted me and that didn't need an occasional beef injection. I wanted a girl that preferred sushi over beef. I wanted to be good enough. More importantly, I desired to be the only one. I believed in one true love, I'd seen it work for my parents and I hoped it'd work for me one day.

I never thought my dream romance would include a constant huddle of boys trying to join in and some of whom were clearly winning. Like the football quarterback who just kissed Hazel on the cheeks. This had to change. I had to tell Hazel it was either me or the football team. Only I was afraid. She'd probably choose the later.

Unfortunately, I had some football players of my own to attend too. Some cute and ugly boys weren't getting the hint that I wanted them to leave me alone. And I didn't want to be mean to them. They kept coming up to me and hitting on me. I fake-numbered them every time, but guilt spread through me. Why can't I just say no and that I'm gay and not interested.

A boy with big ears came over and sat right next to me, not leaving me much room to breath. "Hey, Mackenzie right. You're the new cheerleader."

"No I'm just wear this for Halloween. Want to get an early start." Not caring enough right now to hide my sarcasm.

The big-eared guy laughed, not getting the hint I wanted him to go away. Usually sarcasm can get rid of unwanted people. "Hey, how'd you learn how to do the backflip so many times in a row? I can do a front flip."

"I can do a front flip too." I said, again with the sarcasm.

A boy next to him laughed, as if it was the funniest thing ever. This guy was gorgeous though, he could even hold a candle to my brother and Travis in the looks department. But he was a football player, with huge muscles. Unless they were boobs and not man boobs, it didn't do a thing for me.

Since neither of them seemed to want to go away any time soon I added just as a way to waste time, "My mom's a gymnastics and dance teacher. She trained me since I was young."

"That's so cool." The dorky one said.

The cute one laughed and played with his bushy hair, as if he was a Shetland sheepdog. "Just get her digits."

I told some bogus number with one of the area codes of New York City.

The cute boy overheard me and laughed, but the other one never caught on and they finally left, leaving me in peace, at least for a few minutes.

I smiled politely while another semi -cute boy made boring conversation. I nodded while simultaneously trying to get Hazel's attention to get the hell out of here. She ignored me, sitting a few feet away by the outdoor water fountain while batting her long eyelashes and wide hazel eyes at the boys, casually touching them from time to time.

I wanted to be the only one she flirted with, the only one she winked at; without football players or pimply face nerds. I was sick of being stuck in some heavy road congestion just to get a chance to talk to Hazel.

Also, Hazel's flirting with all these dudes was turning me off big time. Luckily, there might not be any action between us later due to time restraints. It was almost twelve o'clock, my curfew time. If it was a fairytale, my backpack would turn into a pumpkin and take me home. Actually that'd be awesome. Once again, real life is not like the Disney movies. The farthest thing from real life I believe.

Plus, it was freezing cold out here and I only had on a cheerleading uniform and no coat, since I'd forgotten it at home.

"I understand you gave Mike a fake number. Any chance I can get a real one?"

He was cute, model cute with long black hair pulled up in a ponytail and thick eyelashes and high cheekbones. But it didn't matter. I'd never be interested in a guy. Only Zac Efron could make-out with me, but even that would be the farthest I'd take it.

For some odd reason, the boy made his move. Leaning in to give me a kiss I moved fast, making sure he only ended up giving me a kiss on my left cheek.

Finally! I got Hazel's attention. She stormed over to us, glaring at the cute boy. "What are you doing with my girlfriend?"

That was news to me. When did I become her girlfriend? Five minutes ago, she was flirting with what seemed to be the entire football team.

Hazel flipped the boy off with one hand and then pulled me along my arm with the other one. Sharply! "Damn, that hurts," I said, trying to take her firm grip of my arm. But she wasn't budging.

"That boy was all over you. Its okay to flirt now and then, but you're mine. Not some sleazy football player with a small dick." She gripped my hand and ignored the people trying to talk to her or me on the way to the parking lot. I know I dated him last year. Nothing there to have fun with, I can see why he wants you, but he can't have you." Finally, I got my wish. Well, at least for the ride home, to be alone with Hazel. It was too late to do anything sexual. Plus, her meg-jealousy was kind of freaking me out. It was sort of cray cray of her.

My parents probably wouldn't want her sleeping over, although they had a good attitude about it last night. I didn't want to push the line.

When we reached my house, Hazel leaned over into the back seat, retrieving a pile of clothes. She handed over a Coors top and some expensive pants and boots for me to wear. Pink and blue colors, something I rarely wear.

Wow. Now I have two rich people to buy me clothes. With Cherry, it was something I wanted to do. But with my so-called girlfriend, it felt weird. Who was I? A Bratz doll? She wanted to dress me up, change me into someone with more fashion sense and more expensive clothes? I wanted to be enough for my own girlfriend.

If she wanted me to change then I should be able to change her. Will I ever get the chance to change Hazel into someone less temperamental and less flirty? Was that possible? I wish there was an outfit for that one or a simple perfume I could lend her.

Chapter Seventeen

The skinny jeans, pink playboy bunny boots and Coors top
Hazel let me borrow was something I'd never be allowed
to wear in a hundred years in my high school in Utah for
numerous reasons.

But obviously perfectly acceptable here, even revered
as Driver's Ed teach and Coach Mr. Phillips gave me a
nod and called out to me as I reached the school doors at
the end of the day, "Best beer around, my granddad owned
a brewery."

"Cool," I mumbled, well it only came out as a
mumble. I repeated the same word with more surety. Why
was Mr. Phillips talking to me? I thought he hated me.

But he wasn't going anywhere. He looked me up and
down, his eyes bulging with appreciation. "Those were
some tight moves; seems like you could win the end of
year cheer competition for our school on your own, hey,
my daughter's way into dance. I'd pay you to teach her
some gymnastics and cheer moves so she can make the
team next year. She's a sophomore but her Mom doesn't

want her trying out until next year…" he just kept going on and on.

"…Anyway I'll have my wife call you up. Look you up in the book." I decided not to remind him I'm brand new and shouldn't be in any book unless the office somehow got my number. And everything's online now, anyway.

I wanted to shut him up somehow, but wasn't sure how to do it. I needed to pull the brakes on this conversation before I missed the ride to the mall with Hazel. Mercedes was driving. No way would she wait a long time for me.

"I'll get you too hooked up…for real" he said.

I swallowed a laugh at his word usage.

I never had a teacher figure address me as a friend before but I rather enjoyed the attention. Maybe my new stage as a cheerleader had brought me up even in the adult's eyes around here.

I headed out to Mercedes' convertible. Hazel sat on the back lining of the backseat just like a cat would. It was actually warm enough weather, a break between all the snow and rain. A wonderful break!

I hated I had no money but browse-shopping was fun too. Just hanging around my new girlfriend sounded way fun, even though Mercedes was driving.

I was so excited. I jumped in the back, right next to Hazel, choosing to sit cat-style. We both flew our hands up as Mercedes drove off in her Mercedes. We were going shopping.

Then again I spoke too soon. The car jerked sideways, almost causing me to fall out of the car. I decided to slide down into an actual seat, immediately placing my seatbelt on so that I can live past fifteen. Luckily I'll be sixteen in a week if I ever get enough guts to get back behind the wheels of a car if Mr. Phillips approved.

That might not be for another year or so. Of course, he seemed to be warming up to the idea of me. He asked me to help his daughter after all. That takes a lot of trust, even though it didn't include operating any kind of heavy machinery.

We had shopped for hours now and my feet seemed like they were going to fall off. They hurt so badly. I wanted them to fall off.

"This shirt is tight," Hazel placed the shirt up to the top of my body. "And totally your colors," pink and white being my colors was news to me. My blondish-brown hair must flatter such colors because Hazel was often light on the compliments. It was actually something I'd never even given any thought to until now. Mercedes and Hazel were much more the girly-girl type than Cherry and I.

"Sure is," I said, until I looked at the price tag. I didn't even know shirts could cost so much. Unless you're like in some fancy city, then again we are in the Aspen Heights mall. Those people had money to burn and I clearly didn't. I shook my head fiercely.

"She couldn't pull it off?" Mercedes said, holding out a shirt three sizes too big for me. I wasn't an extra large. I wasn't even a large in juniors. What was Mercedes doing here anyway? Oh I forgot, Hazel's Jag was in the shop. You think a six-figure car built in the last few years would never even need to see the front of a car repair shop. Then again the way she drives, she probably ran over a curb or a pedestrian. No shock there.

Choosing to ignore Mercedes, I said. "I can't afford it so it doesn't matter."

"Five-finger discount," Mercedes said, loud enough for a pre-teen customer to overhear, but she didn't seem to realize what it was and just walked away.

"Quiet," Hazel grabbed the shirt and tugged me into a dressing room with her. Wow. We're going to get nasty in this closet-sized room kind of hot if you ask me.

"Try it on," she handed me the playboy shirt. Almost afraid to touch it, she kept holding it out for me in midair. When I didn't touch it, she placed my hands above my head and started taking of Hazel's Coors shirt and then started to put on the three-digit shirt. When I'd finished, I gasped. It brought out the tan color of my skin and the blonde extensions. Pink was a good color. No scratch that, a great color on me and the black bunny made me look thinner as it hit right across my stomach. Plus, the long sleeves and the expensive quality were breathtaking.

I wanted the shirt more than anything. Sure, playboy bunny doesn't send the right message and I'd have to wash it alone, without allowing my Mom to sneak it into the wash and make some judgmental comment. Not to mention the price, it was obvious this shirt wasn't something I got at a thrift store, where we usually do my clothes shopping.

This was way better than what I could ever find at a thrift store. It says that I'm good enough to be girlfriends with Hazel. I wanted it real bad, but not so sure I could do it. That I could steal from a store. Just wasn't right. I'd feel terrible.

How do I say no to Hazel? I didn't want to compromise my values and do something I'd regret. But I loved Hazel. I think I loved Hazel. And the last thing I wanted was to lose her. What was I going to do?

I made my decision. I took the shirt out of my bag when Hazel wasn't looking and placed it in a pile of clothes that were clothes that didn't fit or look good on other people. Or maybe they were sad like me and just couldn't afford them.

I wondered if I was ever going to be enough for her. Just the way I am. Or would I have to wear fancy three-hundred dollar shirts for the rest of my life.

The next thing that happened surprised me. "I snagged you this. She was too chicken to do it." Mercedes said, pulling out the playboy bunny shirt, the exact one I had on minutes earlier. I can't believe she did that.

Hazel smiled, "Can always count on Mercedes to do the dirty deed."

She pulled out a switchblade, an illegal one, to show how she cut off the security tag. Hazel and Mercedes gave each other a high five.

I wished she had said it like it was a bad thing. But she hadn't. She squealed, grabbed the shirt and then gave it to me. I reluctantly took it from her. Getting really sick of being a Bratz doll that needed to be dressed up, not only that but dressed up with stolen merchandise.

A few hours later, I couldn't get what Mercedes had done for me out of my mind and even though it was more her. I still felt responsible and guilty for having a bag right on the floor worth more than any one item in my bedroom, outside of my bed.

The small pierce of guilt bothered me more than anything. Not because it was unsettling, but because where was the rest of it? Why did it barely concern me I'd allowed Mercedes to steal for me?

Had I done so many things lately that my conscience gave up and took a break. What was wrong with me? I even missed the stabbing pain of guilt I was familiar with when I made decisions that hurt other people. In this case, a store's economy and those who are in charge of the store. And the other teens who will have to have their prices jacked up because I stole.

I only wished the two richest girls in school would use their dad or mom's credit card instead of stealing.

Stealing only seemed right if someone had to eat and was starving.

It wasn't like they needed the money. Kids I grew up with needed the money, some could barely afford the lunch money and needed to be on the free lunch program. Here were girls who had everything. Did they even appreciate what they had?

Or were they just so bored by it, they had to spice up their life somehow? Even taking it to criminal actions, all three of us could be processed as adults. Had been known to happen, usually with more severe things like murder, but still.

Hazel and Mercedes seemed to feel no guilt at all. Were they numb to the fact they were hurting store owners and other customers? Did having all the money one could need, make somebody forget about how they make others feel?

Then again, Cherry had money to burn, lots of money to burn and I'd never seen her do anything the least bit immoral besides littering.

Maybe I should go back to the store and give it back? Maybe Paul or Cherry would have an idea that could help me, but the two of them had spent an awful lot of time together lately and neither of them seemed big on my company.

I reached for the forbidden shirt, hidden underneath my queen mattress pad. It was pretty spectacular. It was already stolen. I mean it can't hurt to at least wear it once or twice, if I didn't, Hazel would think I gave it back to the store or something to that effect and probably try to get me to steal again. Or drop me because I was such a boring girl.

I decided the best compromise I could make was to purchase the same shirt with my savings from babysitting, chores and helping my brother out with his schooling. And casually leave the other one behind in the store's dressing room, taking it out of my purse. It seemed like the best idea I've had in a long time, unless I was just turning crazy from all this pressure.

Being popular was the best ever, but it also meant work. It was hard keeping up the image, hard dating the most popular girl and even more difficult not to drown in guilt. I had to keep myself from being swallowed up in the self-hatred again. For once in my life I liked myself, even loved myself. I didn't want anything to change that, not even the girl who is turning my world upside down. I wanted to keep my ground and not lose myself completely in her, the way I do when she's around.

I called Cherry and we had a long discussion about what happened at the mall. She agreed to help me give the shirt back to the mall. She'd told me she would buy me one for real and just sneak the other one back in the dressing room.

So we did just that.

I felt way better on the car ride home in her Malibu.

"I just want to be enough for her. That's all." I said, placing my hand out the window, the cold shocking me. May have been warm in the morning but now it was freezing.

Cherry bowed her head, "You'll always be enough for me."

"Sorry, but not the same,' her eyes crushed together, looking hurt.

"I mean. We'll never be romantically involved. "

A smile formed on Cherry's, lip, reaching her eyes. "Who knows?"

I half-smiled, she was so funny. I know she didn't feel that way about me. I'd seen the way she looked at my brother like she wanted to jump his bones, as disgusting as the thought of that was. It always seemed to be written all over her face when she was around him.

I forgot how much I loved hanging out with Cherry. I'd missed her cuteness something fierce.

When we got back to my house, there was a big plastic bowl of caramel popcorn on my dresser with two cans of Dr. Pepper, my favorite. I smiled.

With the popular girls, I'd always have to put on a show for them. With Cherry, I can jump on my bed and eat as much caramel popcorn as I want and nobody cared or sat around counting calories.

After jumping on my bed and having a competition to see who could do the highest jump. Of course, I won. Then we picked up one of our favorite ninety movie.

Cherry took a huge handful of popcorn and placed almost all of it in her mouth, dripping half of it on my bed.

I laughed. "Hey."

My cares left behind me as leaves falling far from a tree. I focused on the present moment and I was the happiest I'd been all day.

I may be having the time of life with Cherry and with the popular girls, but with Hazel and her crowd it required more acting. Never felt comfortable like I do with Cherry.

Although, I still remember the passion and juiciness of Hazel kissing me, giving me another injection of her life force, as if her blood dripped into mine, giving me a high I never even experienced, even in my dreams. She charged my lack of energy and afterward I constantly craved for more. But I needed to be sustained by my own blood and oxygen. I needed to be happy when she wasn't around, as well. Not hating myself for making poor decisions.

Maybe I needed someone more like a lesbian version of Cherry, who didn't compromise my values and made me happy with or without her. Of course, things were always better when Cherry was around. Wasn't sure I could say the same about Hazel with her occasional temper and tendency to do things I wasn't comfortable doing.

Cherry was far from perfect but she made me feel perfect just the way I was.

Chapter Eighteen

I sat down at my desk, holding in my hands an invitation to a Halloween party. And not just a run of the mill party but a GC one. I'd never had a Halloween invitation before and it bordered on fancy.

I placed the card back on my dresser, where it had rested for a week; n engraved invitation reading Mackenzie Harper. Me. Yea! I squealed once again with delight.

This was the first party that hadn't involved some kid's parents and wasn't at Chucky Cheese, where the birthday kid didn't even want me there. I highly doubted this was the case this time. Sarah didn't have a mean bone in her body well, maybe one might be mean a small one. Plus, Sarah's handwriting always had smiley faces in place of dots. And she'd only reminded me all week about this party.

The engraved part of the invitation read Sarah Ashlee Ryan requests your attendance at an All Hallows Eve for a scary, good time starting at seven P.M. Call to RSVP.

Sarah had given me this a week ago and told me to be prepared, but I never actually believed it would come so soon. She had told me to leave Halloween open.

I avoided pot all week. Somehow! Barely, I'd managed to avoid it with lame excuses such as needing to get a job soon and testing was common. Mercedes argued, said it was illegal to test underage kids, without their parents approval. She told me to just tell them my parents had declined, something about their religious views. But then I made up some other lie saying my parents would figure it out. They weren't dumb. True but still.

After all, the working age was sixteen and my birthday was today. It was actually quite the perfect excuse and the perfect time to get a job. A pretend job! Because my parents refuse to let me work until after I graduate college, how they're going to enforce that, I had no idea.

Everything was going okay with Cherry. Better than okay. It was Hazel that kept asking me why I had to spend so much time with Cherry. Hazel said the last word with a sneer spread across her lips and a voice of disgust.

I'd stared at the invite for hours, going over and over in my mind that I'd arrived. I was one of the popular kids. That fact finally hit me hard. I wanted to dance around in my room, but I settled on turning on some upbeat music and singing to it, hoping nobody was around to listen. If someone overheard me, besides my family, my popularity may go out the window. Fortunately, Paul's music was hella-loud, as usual.

In less than an hour, my family and I were finally having a celebratory dinner of my favorite, spaghetti and meatballs for me having made the cheerleading squad.

It was six P.M. on the dot and time to go down for dinner. I rushed down the stairs to see my family. Paul held a large pink gift while my Mom waved a pomp pomp around.

We all sat around the table, diving into the spaghetti and meatballs and cheesy garlic bread.

Cherry was the only one who was late and Hazel made some excuse about needing to help Sarah get ready for the Halloween party. Guess it wasn't an excuse, but still, my celebratory dinner was important. And my two favorite friends, one of them being a possible girlfriend, weren't here yet.

Still I never figured out if Hazel was my girlfriend or not. So I assumed that was a no. Since she kept dodging the question every time I tried to ask while flirting with anybody in public she desired. So she really had no right to be so iffy about me spending so much time with Cherry, especially when we were just friends.

I slurped down the spaghetti, staring at the full pot of grated cheese I had made for Cherry. Even as a vegetarian, she still ate cheese, just not animal meat. But still she was nowhere in sight.

"Don't you think your mouse costume is a tad bit revealing?" My dad asked me, taking a giant bite of garlic bread, with extra butter. He could eat an entire tub of butter and still not have any weight or cholesterol problems.

"You should see what some of the other girls are wearing." Paul said, coming to my rescue. "She's no more revealing in her cheer uniform. Girls I'd seen in previous Halloween parties only wore bras, whiskers and panties."

He would know. Not sure there was a Halloween Party Paul wasn't invited too, including Sarah's party tonight. Sarah seemed to have a thing for him? But then again who didn't?

A frantic knock sounded on the front door, causing all of us to jump some. Paul left to go get the door before I even moved. A few minutes later, Paul and Cherry came into the kitchen hand in hand.

At first I was pissed, until I saw tears streaming down Cherry's face,

I immediately got up and hugged her without even a thought passing through me. She needed my help. For once, she needed me and I wanted to be there for her no questions asked. I hugged her while she sobbed and didn't make much sense. Paul kept patting her back and saying, "Everything will be okay."

My parents chose to join in and it was like having a huge family hug. They dropped their dinner and came to comfort her. Their hearts were big even if their income was relatively small compared to those in the GC.

"My uncle hates my Moms." That was the only sentence I could make out. "He always says rude things about them like they were tuna-lovers who don't deserve to live."

Now she sounded clear. Almost too clear. I was shocked, shuffling back a few feet from the circle. What the hell was she talking about? She never told me she had two Moms'. I mean it made sense. They were destroyed in a arson fire, a hate crime. All the pieces of the puzzle fit together. Why did I not realize that before?

My dad gets more excited about same-sex rights than I do, his smile could light a dark room. He gave me a sideways hug and whispered, "I love you no matter what." Too bad her mothers weren't around to tell her the same thing. Too bad her Uncle was around willing to spend money on her, but not willing to support it with love. Money can't buy love, and love can't buy money. The two had absolutely nothing to do with one another. But if I had to choose today, I would choose love because having to fight with Paul or whomever over the one shower in our house was so much better than having someone who hated me or my Moms. It wasn't fair.

Finally noticing the shock of those around here, Cherry stopped still. She explained while my mom handed her a box of tissues. She started to dry her eyes, "Yep, my Mom Sue was artificially inseminated with sperm that belonged to some random attorney who was trying to pay for law school, but didn't want any kids."

My dad lovingly patted Cherry on the back, "You'll always be an accepted member of our family. Just the way you are."

My mom shook with fury, "How can he treat his niece in such a manner and expect to one day stand before god with so much hate in his soul."

Cherry left the room abruptly, almost running into a standing vase on the way out. I followed her.

We ended up in the corner, with a waterfall that would be soothing under normal circumstances.

"I wish my Aunt and Uncle were like your parents," Cherry said, this time keeping in her tears. Her sea-green eyes twinkled with fright and unhappiness. It was clear a huge dent rested in her heart, I wondered why I'd never seen it before. Maybe that was why she kept her distance from clubs and sports and from most people. She was hurting and as her best friend, guilt tore me up inside. I should've noticed she was hurting so badly.

I reached in and hugged her, feeling safe and protected; which was odd during the circumstances. I also wanted to keep her safe and protected forever in my arms. "What are they like? You rarely talk about them." I asked her.

"My Uncle doesn't call them same-sex rights. He calls them same-sex jokes. He was never accepting of my Mom, his sister-in-law, always made fun of her."

Cherry and I had a long talk. We ended up sitting down on the living room couch for what seemed like minutes. She told me about her Moms and how they were murdered by arson in the vintage bookstore they owned together. It was a terrible hate crime by some religious freaks who disapproved of their so-called lifestyle.

When I looked at my cowgirl watch, five hours had passed, three of those hours I should've been over at Sarah's with Mercedes and Hazel setting up. Hazel was going to kill me. I'd tell her it was an emergency, but she didn't seem to care about my emergencies so much.

Cherry and I hugged each other goodbye in Sarah's driveway, since she had offered to drop me of on her way to face her Uncle and give him a piece of her mind. She was going to face her demons and then head over to the party

She drove away fast, seeing something in the distance that seemed to bother her.

I turned around, noticing what she was avoiding.

"What the hell are you doing?" Hazel called, coming out from the side of Sarah's house, after decorating a tree with tiny witch-hat paper creations. "You're three hours late because of her," the way she said 'her' sent chills rocketing up my spine "She better be dying or close."

Yea, her Ghost just gave me a ride, I wanted to say. Instead I said, "I'm here, aren't I?"

"Yea three hours late," Hazel huffed and stood next to Mercedes, placing her hands on her hips.

"Sorry." I managed to say, even though I didn't mean it at all. Realizing just how bossy and controlling Hazel can be at times. Why did she care so much what I did with Cherry? Maybe she knew about her Moms and suspected Cherry was gay, but Cherry's not. So why did Hazel care so much?

I was going to point out she was supposed to be at my celebratory dinner but refused after taking one look at her. Hazel was scowling, if looks could burn, I'd be ashes. I wanted to make it through my first real party without turning into a ghost.

Chapter Nineteen

I stood in the driveway, frozen in time and space.
Mercedes came out the front door, standing right in front
of Hazel, as if trying to protect her. I'd clearly pissed off
the wicked witch of the East and the West, only they're
from the same GC multi-million dollar neighborhood and
they were used to getting their way.

I wondered at that moment what I ever saw in Hazel in
the first place. She wasn't even all that beautiful and her
trashy nurse's uniform only made her look well, trashy.
She didn't even possess the boobs to fill it out and her legs
were kind of chicken-y. I had way overestimated her looks
and way underestimated the dire problems with her
personality.

"Let's just go inside and try to enjoy the party," Hazel
said, with ice-cube water running through her voice.

I followed the two of them inside, but I didn't feel
welcome. And I especially didn't feel special when I saw
Maiko there in a pumpkin costume. She looked pretty

silly. Maybe you didn't have to be popular to be invited to this party.

Searching around the large front foyer, as if it was built just for a party, I noticed everyone seemed to be invited, including Cherry and her senior butch friend, Sam, huddled together in the far corner, over by the water fountain.

It bothered me. I wanted to be special, feel special for once, while others were sitting at home being uninvited. Then again, I didn't want anyone to be hurting or to be left out or to feel as horrible as I used to feel.

Maybe for once, I realized, that was the way it should be. Why should anyone get excluded for being different or shy or picked on. Sarah knew what she was talking about by inviting the whole class. She had the right perspective. She's always had the right perspective. She's not even Christian, but she's got the meaning of Christ's love down pat, while Mercedes claimed to be Catholic and seemed to have no idea.

"Why did you have to invite everyone and their cat?" Mercedes said to an approaching Sarah, wearing angel wings and a halo, pointing to a person walking on all-fours, meowing like a cat, even though they weren't dressed as one.

I headed straight for the bathroom, leaving the door partway open in case someone needed to use the restroom. I needed to cool down and check on my makeup. My mouse costume looked way modest compared to Hazel's nurse's uniform. It covered me well, showing off my newly shaved and tan legs. I've always tanned easily and kept it. We have Native American blood in our family.

Speaking of blood, two voices interrupted me as they came closer. I recognized both of them so I ducked behind the shower curtain. "I'm breaking the blood bond." I looked in the crack between the shower curtain and the crevices in the wall, the voice came from Mercedes and she sounded firm in whatever the hell she was talking about.

"No need to be dramatic. We don't know what's going on?" Hazel said, being the voice of reason while applying more mascara on her already long lashes.

'What the hell was a blood bond?' I whispered quietly to myself. I heard a sharp movement, worried someone had overheard me. But Sarah's bathroom was gigantic and hiding in the three person whirlpool tub with a massive off-black laced shower curtain was practically foolproof. When I heard Mercedes' voice again, I relaxed some.

"There's no way Cherry's getting away with this again?"

Again? What could she have possibly done? Cherry couldn't hurt a mosquito, even if it had stung her repeatedly.

"She's not stealing another one of your girlfriends; she can't get away with it." I could see Mercedes flipping her hair before applying more purple lip gloss. Purple was so not her color and she wore a purple shirt with hot pink earrings with a side ponytail. Was she trying to be some horribly-dressed eighties chick?

And why would Cherry steal me? We're not dating. She's not even gay? What did these two girls take before I came to the party? They had to be high? Maybe too much ecstasy and they hallucinated Cherry doing things she could never have done.

"I'll handle it."

"No, you won't. You won't do anything. You never do. I'm not afraid of Sam or Mackenzie. I'll make sure Cherry gets her karma." Mercedes sighed loudly. "I want this Mackenzie person off the squad, out of my spot and away from you. And I'm going to make it happen with or without you."

I accidently tripped over a shower brush and fell, making a huge noise. Stubbing my toe, ouch that hurt.

But not as much as it did when the shower curtain opened, revealing two angry girls. People I would have died weeks ago trying to impress. Now I wanted them both to disappear out of my life and I didn't like the way they wanted to exact revenge on my best friend; the one person who had never been mean to me.

"Are you cheating on my girl with that Cherry person?"Mercedes turned to me with sour distaste in her voice.

I couldn't answer. My selective muteness came back full force. I didn't know what to say even though the answer to me was clear. Of course, I'd never done anything to Cherry. They were both talking like the criminally insane or at least the insane out for revenge.

"See. I told you." Mercedes said, storming out of the bathroom, and slamming the door behind her with a big thump.

I started shaking and there wasn't anything I could do about stopping it. I trembled all over and shook my head to signal no. But I was back to being a mute and couldn't defend myself. I hated both of them for making me feel this way, even if they played a huge role in my recent popularity.

I no longer wanted anything to do with Hazel, I didn't want to be her girlfriend and I also hated the idea of having any real contact with her from here on out.

Hazel looked at me coldly, obviously feeling the same way. She crossed her eyes and looked at me as if I was a shadow and she couldn't quite make out who I was. That maybe I wasn't who she thought I was all along, either. I wanted to explain, explain why I was spying. Explain what was really going on with Cherry. But I had no strength, my muteness crept back in and my social anxiety took hold of my body like ivy-plant vines attaching to my neck and choking me. I had gone back to the way I used to feel around her.

Finally Hazel left. I waited a few minutes to get some of my breath and energy back and intended to run straight for the door but something stopped me. Someone stopped me. It was a voice. "Why's the dyke kissing Cherry?"

I followed the voice into the front room, where everyone stared at a large flat screen television. Some cheered while Sam and Cherry moved from their waterfall area to see what all the commotion was about.

"Oh no," I heard Cherry's cry. I immediately wanted to beat up whomever it was that made her sound so broken inside.

It didn't take too long to find the culprit. A smiling Mercedes stared at the TV, her hand holding a few DVD's, while standing close to the disc player. From the crowd's ewes and ahs, she had obviously found the one she wanted.

I pushed my way up to the front, pushing past the pumpkin Maiko who would've let me go before her, but I forced my way. The short buzz-cut of Sam's hair and Cherry's long strawberry pig-tails were in an embrace, what appeared like a lip-locking embrace? Yep, there was definitely tongue.

Was Cherry bi and I didn't realize it. Was I really that dense about my best friend? The one who noticed that first day on the lake my attraction to girls, maybe she noticed because she was doing the same thing. Why had that not occurred to me before? With all of Mercedes snide remarks, Cherry's secretiveness and her lack of boy-seeking attention. How could I be so blind? Was I that preoccupied with Hazel?

Sarah's voice brought me out of my thoughts, "How could you do this? Cherry used to be one of us. We were like the Scooby gang, but a hotter version and no dog." Sarah spat out to Mercedes, her face aflame.

"Aren't you going to do something? This is wrong." Sarah asked Hazel, who only shrugged, staying put.

Sarah moved rapidly to an end table, picking up a DVD remote and shutting off the DVD player and then retrieving another remote to shut off the television."Party's over." Sarah called out over and over.

For the few stragglers, she screamed. "Cops coming, everyone out, including you two." She pointed to Mercedes and Hazel.

Then she turned to me. "You stay." She told me, as if I was her puppy dog, but I think she was protecting me, so it didn't bother me.

After a few minutes, when I saw Paul leave with Cherry and Sam, I raced out to go check on them, but Sarah chased after me and held me back in the foyer.

"I'm so sorry," Sarah said.

"Why have you stayed friends with them for so long?" I asked her.

"Because I believe in forgiveness."

"What about Cherry?"

"Cherry never needed me. That girl's strong. I never stopped being her friend though," One of Sarah's curls dropped from on top of her head. She played with the curl nervously.

I turned away from Sarah without saying another word. My brother didn't need my help with Cherry, but I had to see if she was okay. The minute I stepped out, I noticed the sharp, cold breeze.

Cherry rarely needed anybody picking her up, her mood was often upbeat and she always saw the positive side of things. Yes, I wanted to be the one to help her, but I wanted to be the strong one, and I didn't mean physically. I wanted to get my shit together, I wanted to stop hanging out with friends who use pot and steal as everyday activities. Or who excluded or made fun of people because they were different.

Knives tearing into my back would be more pleasant than this wave of mixed emotions running through my body. I wanted to scream at them to stop, make Hazel leave Cherry alone. But I was back. Back to being unable to speak, only air coming from my mouth.

I hated bullies. I'd spent enough of my life ducking those kinds of people and shedding useless tears for people who didn't matter. I was done. I couldn't do this anymore. I couldn't sit idly by while Hazel and Mercedes poisoned other people, deliberately to hurt them. Even if she denied

it and said she wasn't doing anything wrong, Hazel got
something out of putting other people down, saying
they're not worthy and not on her level.

I'd have to sort out my confused thoughts later, now
was the time to retain my voice and give it to the person
who deserved my vengeance.

I couldn't find Mercedes so I approached Hazel, who
stood on the porch as if admiring Cherry's and Sam's
earlier walk of shame.

I glared, wishing my eyes would burn some sense into
her. "How could you do this to Cherry?"

"I didn't do anything wrong. It was all Mercedes," she
said matter-of-factly, wearing an innocent expression.

"Well you didn't do anything to stop it now, did you?"

Hazel only laughed, amusement sparkling in her dark
eyes.

Mercedes called Hazel over from her Mercedes, so I
left in a huff before Hazel could.

Entering Cherry's open front door, I found out all too
soon that it was too late to help Cherry or Sam. Cherry was
passed out on her front couch with Paul hovering over her
and Sam drinking gulps from a bottle of Vodka and then
finally placing the empty bottle back in her bag. She

looked like a boy for the Halloween occasion, unless it was a more permanent solution.

Luckily, Cherry's Aunt and Uncle were nowhere in sight.

"Is she going to be okay?" I asked them both.

Sam shrugged and so did Paul. Neither of them said a word.

Through this whole social expansion experience of mine, I discovered who's worth getting to know and who isn't. Who's worth being around and protecting and who isn't. Who possessed that light inside of them that made them a real human, someone with a big heart and knows that love always rules over power and Cherry was one of those people.

Sarah and Cherry were these people and Sam's never done a thing to hurt me. And even if it ruins my chance to be popular and well-liked, or maybe even to cheer, there was no way in damn that I was going to allow someone to embarrass the only real friend I've ever had. I don't care what her sexuality is. I don't even care she felt the need to hide the truth of her real parents from me. She accepted me the way I was and it was my turn to do the same.

I went back outside. Before I lost my nerve, I yelled to Hazel and Mercedes who smoked some joint by the Mercedes, still on Sarah's property.

"I'm a one-hundred percent Dyke and proud of it." I screamed to Mercedes and Hazel. Sarah stepped out on her porch at the same time and laughed.

Sarah clapped her hands and winked. "Wow the cheerleader finally learned how to best use her lungs."

I was so grateful for Sarah at that moment, I could've kissed her. She was no adorable Cherry, but she was certainly adorable.

"Bye-Bye witches," Sarah said to Hazel and Mercedes, while they got in the car and drove off angrily down the driveway, both flipping their middle fingers out the window. That could very well be the end of that threesome friendship. Hopefully it'd be the end of Hazel's and Mercedes' royal reign, but I doubted it. Sarah would likely be the one cast out of that coven.

Chapter Twenty

My worst fear had happened. Almost everyone at school was treating me like an outcast. It hadn't mattered I'd moved a state away to avoid the catcalls and the bullying. Pretty soon, it could result in violence and there wouldn't be anything I could do to stop it.

I tried to play sick, but my Mom knew about what happened last night because well it seemed like everyone somehow new. Maybe it was broadcasted on local news or maybe Paul just told her.

I asked my Mom if she would homeschool me for the hundredth time and her answer was always the same, "Homeschool kids are weird. You need to have social skills to get along in this world and school was a vital place to start learning those skills." The main thing I learned was how to hide from bullies. I learned social skills from the summer with Cherry and the social therapy group during the summer.

I knew Paul was on my side but I hadn't seen him all morning. Cherry had skipped advanced English, and I wasn't sure if she was mad at me or not. Wasn't sure she was even going to school. I hoped and prayed her Uncle of all people didn't know what had transpired last night.

I looked around for Cherry, and saw her by the coke machine, next to Sam who was kicking the machine. Maybe that's where Cherry learned to dance to her own music. Sam did whatever she wanted and not surprisingly the lunch workers seemed too afraid to say anything, to even look her way, they just seemed to look at each other weird on Sam's behalf.

"Luckily, my Uncle didn't believe Hazel's mom when she told him what happened last night," Cherry said to Sam, while they both sat down on the table next to me. Couldn't figure out what Sam was doing in our lunch, but whatever. The more people the better and people were scared of Sam.

"That's a relief." Sam crossed her legs on the folding lunch chair..

The more people the better to fight the bullies and people responded to Sam, they were afraid of her. So we were safe, for the time being. I crossed my fingers, praying I could make it another two and a half years, with two of the years being without Sam and one being without Cherry. I was literally going to die.

But, I was relieved Cherry was ok and the sight of her beautiful face brought joy to me. She smiled, not wide and goofy like her Cheshire cat smile, but at least she seemed okay.

"You all right?" Cherry asked, licking off some of the cheese on one of her chips.

Figured, Cherry would be worried about other in a time of crisis. "I'd been called almost every name in the book," I stared at my soggy nachos, feeling sorry for myself. The same people who used to worship me called me names now, including the guy with the big ears.

It sucked having popularity and then losing it. But at least it made me realize how shallow popularity was. I never needed popularity, it wasn't important. I never needed the ego boost; it was inside me all along. I had the power to love myself the way I am.

So far this morning I responded to the mean cat-calls in a Cherry fashion with secret flip-offs or pretended not to care. I did care, but not as much as I'd normally care.

"Honey, I'd been called every name in the book. You on the other hand, don't even know half the derogatory terms out there." Sam said it in good spirits, but it almost made me want to cry. How could she be treated so badly, even I had judged her with disdain? When she was clearly a good person, especially since she used to date Cherry? Cherry had the best judge of character I knew. That must mean I was all right too. Sam had Cherry's back, in my book that meant something.

I hoped they weren't still dating? Was I that clueless? They did seem pretty chummy. The idea wigged me out more than I wanted it too. Did I like Cherry?

Funny thing was. Life seemed better in a way than it was weeks ago with all that popularity. People didn't like me for me. They liked some version I created. Cherry liked me all along. It'd be a shame if she was already spoken for.

I searched for the GC popular table, but Hazel and Mercedes were nowhere in sight. The nightmare of me chewing out Hazel at the party came back full force. How could I even forget that night for a second? Nobody had let me forget all day.

Guess my problems were consuming me at least for the time being. I wished I could help Cherry out more. Wait. Maybe there was a way. I needed to ask Sam later how a teenager becomes emancipated. At least that'd get

Cherry's Uncle off her back so she can be away from the homophobic asshole.

I'd bring it up, but they were pretty busy talking and even I was somewhat scared of Sam's reaction. Would she laugh at me? I couldn't take another person laughing at me today.

Sarah came down from the GC table to sit next to me. She shocked me momentarily that I dropped nachos cheese sauce all over my shirt. At least, it was a cheap one I'd gotten at goodwill.

"You okay, girl?"

I nodded.

Sam, Sarah and Cherry saved me from racing to the bathroom and locking myself in until school was over. Screw eating, I could barely look at those soggy nachos on my table. I just wanted to escape.

But it helped. It helped to have friends, true friends around me even if they had their own serious problems to deal with.

I smiled, relieved to have Cherry here with me. She was the greatest friend anyone could hope for; I needed her to know that I went after her. I'd just gotten detained from Sarah, but now wasn't the time to talk about it.

I was sure I could forgive her for lying to me or from keeping such huge secrets from me. Maybe not this fast, but that time will for sure come. I more wanted to know the reason why she felt she couldn't trust me.

I could hardly believe she was lesbian this whole time. I was so dumb for not even picking up on it. She even had two really good excuses including, her Uncle's asshole ways and the horrible hate crimes that took both her mother's away.

I swallowed my words down, not wanting to hurt my friend. Even if she lied to me, she never meant to hurt me. No, that was more of a Hazel thing to do. She didn't care who her actions hurt, just thinking about her sent waves of fear up my spine.

"Going to get some more nacho cheese sauce to go with my chips," Sam said, shaking what was left of her cartoon, a pile of chips. "You guys want?"

I ignored her. Cherry shook her head.

Figured now was my chance. I breathed in deeply, before starting, "You could have told me," I said, not even bothering with the small talk, getting right to the issue, small talk was never my specialty, anyway.

"I know. And I should've." As per usual, Cherry knew what I was talking about without me having to spell it out.

Cherry's usually the one taking care of me. My turn was past due. She needed me and I wouldn't pass up the chance to be there for her. "It's not like I would've judged. But I'm here for you know and I love you all the same." There were so many opportunities for her to tell me. How dense could I be? Maybe she tried to tell me all along, but I wasn't listening. Too wrapped up in Hazel, too self-consumed to pay any attention?

Paul sat down, interrupting the unfinished conversation. Without meaning to, I must have sent him a dirty look, because he said. "What?"

"Nothing," I tried to smile, grateful Paul had decided to leave the GC popular table to sit with us not-so-popular ones.

I think it was official. High school was going to be okay. At least this time I had the power. Had the friends and had the social skills necessary to lift my chin up and ignore the bullies.

I finally knew who I was, a good friend and a good person. And that was all that mattered.

"Loser table," Mercedes and Hazel said in sync as they walked by our table, wearing their cheer uniforms.

"Maybe you shouldn't talk to them that way." Sarah said, sitting down at the lunch table with us, also wearing her uniform. The rest of us stared back and forth at each other, trying to figure out what she was doing sitting with us. With the wide grin on her face directed at Paul, I figured maybe he had something to do with her presence.

"If you still want to be friends with Witch One and Witch Two, you could apologize," Sarah said to me, as if offering me advice but with a joking half-smile.

"No thanks."

Everyone laughed. I appreciated Sarah's half-joking half-serious help, but I didn't want to apologize. I had nothing to apologize for. I spoke the truth; I didn't set out to hurt Hazel. Cherry and Sam were the ones who deserved an apology from Hazel, if any apologizes were going to go around.

Sarah took a bite of one of her cheesy nachos, spilling some of it on her cheerleading vest. Jealousy tugged at my heart, I wanted to be wearing my outfit. Just my luck to miss out on the one activity that made me the happiest, well gymnastics and dance were what made me the happiest. Cheerleading came a distant second. Could never get completely over all the nerves with how my voice sounded.

I missed wearing my cheer uniform, but I didn't miss Hazel and Mercedes bossing me around and encouraging me to do illegal activities. My moral code was back in tact and I intended to keep it that way.

Hazel stomped her way back to our table and said in a loud enough voice for the entire cafeteria to overhear. "Sarah, you need to return your uniform now."

"You can't just cut someone off, just because you don't like them?"

Hazel pointed to Miss Aimee, who for some reason did not sit with the other teachers in the lounge like the other adults did. She nodded and went back to talking to a few wannabes she sat with. "It's already done. I got Miss Aimee's permission."

"She's Hazel, she can do whatever she wants," Sam said sarcastically and somewhat seriously. We all knew she was right, at least when it came to Miss Aimee, who allowed Hazel to be queen bee.

"Well this is my outfit and I'll take it off when I want."

"Fine. Suit Yourself."

"Bye now," Paul said, as Hazel walked away. Hazel cringed at his words, unlike most, Hazel respected Paul's opinion.

She came back over to speak to Paul directly, "Of course, you're always welcome on any team here at Aspen

Heights." As if Hazel was the person who decided who could be on what team in all of the school.

He ignored her and said to the table "Why don't you start a gymnastics or and dance team."

Hazel laughed, and when she finally left. We all shrugged it off.

***

But we ended up doing just that. A week later we had a performance scheduled for half-time during basketball tomorrow. Hazel and Miss Aimee tried to protest, but Miss Romero was a favorite of the Principal so we got our way.

Over the past week, we had enjoyed planning our own gymnastics slash dance team. Ms. Romero agreed to start the team with us so we had auditions and found out what an amazing dancer Maiko was, even though she was the only one who showed up. Her and the principal daughter, Glitter, who he wanted me to take under her wing. Rumor had it Mercedes threatened all the girls in school who had even thought about trying out with suspension, like she even had that kind of power. She pretended to though and that was apparently enough to scare them away.

But we had to have six people so Paul offered to be the sixth, since it was his idea.

"Why don't we send Cherry to the baseball field and keep Paul, he has more rhythm," Sam said, at the lunch table.

"Hey, she's a piano player. I'm working with her. She's got more rhythm coming out of her ear then even this person right here does," Sarah said, pointing to herself.

"Only because you want to get in good with a certain brother around here somewhere," I teased.

Paul had just arrived at the table, but he pretended he hadn't heard anything. "What?" he asked, but everyone shook their head, besides Sarah, who was too busy blushing.

The six of us had become inseparable over the past week. We hung out after school and at lunch.

"I just hope we'll be ready for tomorrow," Cherry said nervously, biting on her fingernails.

Hazel walked by us at that moment so we all shut up. Our first performance was going to be later tonight during half-time at the basketball team. She had to be pissed about Sarah leaving the JV cheerleading squad, but she acted like she wasn't. But wasn't that all Hazel did. Was act?

Hazel had pretended to love and care about me, but she only wanted my skills for the team and for me to step in line. But once I stopped stepping in line and doing what she wanted me to do, she threw me up like a hot cup of Tabasco. Was I just garbage to her or someone she cared about? It was too hard to tell the difference.

Mercedes was happy, now the JV captain, and they got some pretty girl from French class to join, but she had less rhythm than Cherry. I sneaked in to watch them practice one day. She probably had to stay in the back to keep from screwing up everyone else and from anyone actually noticing that her moves were off by half-a-second at least.

Cherry was too kind to not tell me, 'I told you so.' But I felt one was due. She warned me over and over that she was bad news and I never listened. What the hell was I thinking? Not even listening to the one person who's never left my side, outside the family.

Cherry never stopped being there for me, if anytihng I pushed her away. Life was great with her at the beginning of the school year, before Hazel arrived. Way better than last year. I never had to starve myself because I chose not to eat in the toxic-infested bathrooms. I thought I wanted popularity. I thought I needed popularity, to prove I was valuable and important. I don't need fake friends who only liked me for my popularity or makeover. Sam and Cherry, well particuarly Cherry liked me before, just the way I am and so did my family. I just needed to catch up to them.

Cherry was talking nonstop, making me feel at ease as she smiles often, revealing her two adorable dimples. I listened intently to her every word, imaging what it'd be like if she suddenly leaned over and kissed me.

Cherry's just so beautiful, words don't even begin to portray her accurately. Another person might walk by her and see an ordinary teenage girl who could use a few pounds. But when I look at her she is the most beautiful person I've ever met. She's an acid trip of beauty I've never experienced in my life. And it isn't her face, her eyes or even her legs. It was everything rolled up in one, even the freckles on her chin and the semi-Pinocchio length of her nose, are gorgeous in ways words can never fully comprehend. She was gorgeous on the outside because her beauty radiated from the inside out.

Maybe as far as the world or my high school was concerned, Hazel was way out of Cherry's league. But to me, it was the other way around. Pretty isn't on the outside like a flat screen, it encompassed so much more. And Cherry was real, only becoming more beautiful as I got to know her. Sure she was flawed, always having a sticky blow pop in her mouth and leaving the gum everywhere. But even her flaws made her who she was and I loved her just the same.

Ever since I found out she's lesbian, I can't stop thinking what it would be like to be with her romantically. Never realized how much I was holding back with her. How much of a crush I really had on her? I had wondered why those times she hung out with my brother had gotten on my nerves so much. Now I know. Now the Sam and Cherry flirting was getting on my nerves in the worse way.

All I ever wanted was to be was a normal teen. I wished to get invited to parties and have friends to sit with at lunch. Somehow I got what I wanted and I just wanted more and couldn't stop myself. When I was with Cherry, I was happy, no I was more than happy. I felt alive for the first time in my life. I can't....can't for the life of me fathom why I wanted more.

I just couldn't stand looking in from the outside anymore, never getting to know the real person, not even knowing who I was in comparison. I never realized, until now, that it was only Cherry I needed and wanted. Getting close to her was the best part of my life so far. I was falling in love. When she was around, everything else seemed weightless and far away.

I could handle losing Hazel, but losing Cherry would kill a part of me. So I wasn't sure how to tell her all these things without worrying about the terrible risk of losing her or changing our friendship. Wasn't sure I could handle that? So I kept silent for now.

Twenty-One

It was the day of the performance. I needed to stay focused on our morning practice, our last practice before the dance at the basketball half-time show tonight, but I couldn't focus. All I kept thinking about was how beautiful Cherry looked in her juicy fruity sweatpants and her forest green tank-top. Watching her was making me mess up my moves.

The main difference between this morning practice and all the other ones were none of us screwed up our moves. Besides me!

Without Paul's horrible lack of rhythm and with all the extra help Cherry had received from Sarah was clearly starting to pay off. Cherry wasn't throwing me off because she was doing things wrong, it was because I couldn't stop thinking about her.

Nothing seemed right to me. I wasn't sure I could go any longer without knowing how Cherry really felt about me I wanted to know if she was still dating Sam, not that I would blame her at all. Sam was confident, unafraid and even attractive in a butch way. She wasn't anything like me, so it wouldn't make much sense if Cherry liked me, after being with her.

Sarah faced the five of us, her back against the bleachers. "Glitter, you are perfect, keep it up." She then glanced at me, wearing a frown, but said nothing.

I realized I'd been sucking at this but Cherry's every move bewitched me. The toss of her long braids swaying with her decent moves. She tried so hard and every move was right on, while I just tripped over my left foot, landing on my ass.

Ouch! That killed. Everyone looked my way, including the few tall, skinny boys playing basketball before school. How embarrassing could I be? I was such a freak! This routine was child's play compared to what I was used to. I had to talk to Cherry even if I was scared to hell of losing her or changing our close friendship.

Sarah cornered me at the end of practice just as the first bell rang. The rest of the group left, except Cherry. I stared at her as she jumped from her spot and grabbed her gym bag from the bleachers, starting to rustle through it. Not bothering with going to the locker room because the boys had left, she hurried and changed right there and then.

Her bra and underwear weren't laced or matching; in fact she had white granny panties on, but I didn't care. She was the most beautiful semi-naked person I'd ever seen.

"Oh my, could you be more obvious?" Sarah asked.

"Huh. What?" I asked, responding to Cherry's good-bye wave with both of my hands.

"You have a major thing for that girl," Sarah nodded in Cherry's direction as she left the gym, the door closing behind her.

"Who?" I tried to play dumb. Hearing those words out loud made them too real, it scared me. I wasn't ready to admit to anything.

"You know who? The one you stared at instead of doing moves you can normally do in your sleep?"

"I didn't stare at anybody."

Sarah grinned, for the first time I noticed her white - colored braces on her bottom teeth. "Come on. Be serious."

All the heat ran to my face and no words seemed to be able to fix this. I didn't want anyone knowing I liked Cherry, especially since Cherry didn't even know. "A—"

"Don't worry. I noticed her crush on you a couple months ago and she couldn't deny it any more than you could, even though she's a much better liar than you."

Sarah turned around, leaving me to an empty gym with my thoughts.

Did Cherry really like me back? We had lots of fun together. She gave me a key, not sure what the key meant, but it seemed valuable. She warned me about staying away from Hazel, even though I never listened. She always had my back. She even seemed jealous of my time with Hazel and Mercedes on occasion.

What did all this mean? She had had a crush on me for months. That couldn't be true, could it? I couldn't fathom actually being able to date someone who was also a best friend. I knew so much about her and I loved her. Had she felt romantic toward me this whole time?

I decided to skip first period, not ready to see Sarah, Cherry or Hazel in Advanced English. I sat down on the bleachers, getting out of the way as the gym started to fill up with a first period gym class with sophomore boys and girls starting to play basketball against one another.

Later that evening, right before the half-time performance, Cherry pulled me aside.

"I don't have that much time. So I have to make this quick and more direct than I want. But I have always wanted you, hoped you would one day feel the same way about me," Cherry took out a crystal key necklace from under her brown dressy shirt.

My mouth opened, it was an exact replica of the one she gave me. "It opens up the key to that box you dropped that one time, the most important things I still have from my Moms. The only things besides the Malibu left from the fire."

It sounded like it was a key to her heart, and I'd had it for a long time. Why did it take me so long to realize what I had right in front of me?

"Since the fire, my Malibu and that box was all that mattered. Not anymore."

Then I did something I never had the courage to do to anyone. I saw her rose colored lips and pressed mine against hers. I'd dreamt of such a moment ever since I knew what kissing was. But still my best fantasies couldn't begin to compare to the real thing. The passion and warmth of her lips made me want to scream in joy. I was kissing Cherry Adams. Better yet. I was kissing my best friend and the person I loved with every beat of my heart. The effect was nothing like Hazel's kisses.

"Come on girls," Sarah called us down from the gym floor.

We didn't perform our moves flawlessly, well maybe we was close. My double back flip at the end helped matters. But our energy and enthusiasm got the crowd going and they loved us. They probably could see how close on the gym and out of the gym our relationships went. The six of us seemed to just have a spark.

We were done in what seemed like seconds. The audience roared with cheering and clapping, including some of the members of the cheerleading squad, minus two. Mercedes and Hazel frowned while trying to get their cheer members to quiet down.

Three of the JV cheerleaders ignored Mercedes calling after them to stop, as if they were her dogs, and instead sat with us on the bleachers, begging Sarah to be a part of our dance team.

Sarah nodded happily, "The more the better."

I mouthed a thank you to the Coach and then to Paul, who left his side and came over to congratulate us.

We not only have a dance team but we got three more members, all in their cheerleading uniforms. For now! Soon they'll have one of our team's future leotards. Never thought I could be so happy. I was doing what I loved and was with whom I loved.

Cherry hugged me and said, "Congrats." My endorphins raised and happiness spread throughout me, I felt like I was finally safe and at home in a public space.

When she let go, I thirsted for the kind of happiness that only came from her. Every moment with her was better than thinking about her. Every moment with her was a natural high. I didn't need drugs or the thrill of shoplifting. Most importantly, with Cherry, I could be me and that was enough. That was always enough.